SUNRISE

Rodger Morris

Copyright © 2017 Rodger Morris
All rights reserved
First Edition

PAGE PUBLISHING, INC.
New York, NY

First originally published by Page Publishing, Inc. 2017

ISBN 978-1-63568-573-2 (Paperback)
ISBN 978-1-63568-574-9 (Digital)

Printed in the United States of America

PREFACE

This book Sunrise is an attempt by this writer to tie all the sentences of my life onto one page. The importance of the Sunrise has inspired me all of my life for I see God in each and every one. I rise early every morning and step outside to greet the day with anticipation. The Sunrise starts my day off on not only the right foot but in the right frame of mind. I encourage you all to write your own stories for one day you will get to the point in your life when you will lose your ability to remember all the details and names of those who walked with in this journey we call life. My attempt in this writing is relay to you all the many steps that must be taken to get us to our stations in life. Some stories are humorous while some are sad while others are told to show us all the moral of the stories. Some stories are told in an attempt to insert oneself into a situation and discover you yourself have faced these same situations. Join me and try to find your own Sunrise in life for God intended us to see his face.

ACKNOWLEDGEMENTS

I first want to acknowledge God for he is the creator of all. Next I would tell of how much my upbringing has played a large part of the creation of this book. Mr. Dee Ozment my scout leader and later principle played a huge role in my life. Mr. Russell Caldwell pried my eyes open to the wonders of the passions I possess and helped me to appreciate my family. To Diane Inman whose support and encouragement was invaluable in the writing of this book. To my wonderful wife and three daughters who accompanied me on this wonderful journey. And to the many friends I have rubbed elbows along this trip they call life.

FOREWORD

When we first moved to our rural neighborhood, my husband reported one day that he had met the Morris boys on a nearby farm. He was smiling because the three boys reminded him of his own brothers out rabbit hunting. Down through the years, our family had many connections with this neighboring family. The youngest brother (not then rabbit hunting) would be in the same grade school classroom as our youngest child.

Rodger especially held our interest, however, because he and his girl friend often fished down at our pond. When they were married in a nearby country church and our daughter sang at their wedding, we claimed to have helped that courtship along. We enjoyed watching their three adorable blond daughters first in their little Easter bonnets and pretty Christmas dresses. Next we watched them grow up and excel in school and college. Because of the many community connections at school and church, I thought I knew Rodger well. Then Rodger brought over the manuscript for this book.

From his account of his life, I found out so much I did not know about his life—his passions and his experiences both as a child and while he was out seeing the world during his four years in the U.S. Navy. I envied all those visits he made to other countries and appreciated his enjoyment of these other cultures. Whether it was eating a meal cooked over the fire in a huge pot by a Peace Corps couple in Africa, shopping in. shops in Pakistan, riding a camel, or crossing the Equator, Rodger helped me travel there too. I felt the overwhelming emotions as his ship returned to Charleston, SC, and he saw his young wife waiting for him there. I've seen their dining table in their present home, but now I know the table's story.

I knew Rodger liked humor and practical jokes, and now I know some of the stunts he has pulled including his favorite and mine when he made an unexpected visit to his fiancé in nursing school in St. Louis and phoned her from the parking lot having her look out the window to see what the weather was like outside that window.

I knew Rodger had experienced bi-polar episodes, and perhaps that helps explain the intense awareness of the beauty all around him that he shares with us. His hobby of collecting Indian relics is enhanced by his visualization of the first owners of those antiquities. Refinishing furniture, coaching softball, meshing with shipmates or coal mine buddies, and participating in family life are all experienced with pleasure and excitement. What I did not understand was the recurring battles he fought with deep depression on the other end of the emotional scale. I admire his openness in sharing these difficult times because of his desire to help others who suffer with this disease. I'm grateful for more understanding of what this disorder means to someone living with it.

Rodger calls himself a simple man, and yet his life has been rich and complex. He offers an example of living through both adversities and triumphs and being able to look forward to the sunrises yet to come.

Mom & Dad

1
MY STORY

My story begins on February 19, 1953, in Herrin, Illinois. I was born to Geither and Mary Morris, being one of three brothers. My life was a simple life, one in my father's 320-acre farm in deep Southern Illinois. Life there was not complicated. We had to work to make the farm life worthwhile for us all. My mother was a homemaker, and my dad worked construction as well as farmed and raised hogs and cattle. My mother had a heavy load raising three boys and caring for the house and a husband on that farm. She did all these things with not a single complaint. I can remember my mother singing as she did the housework or the washing and how she seemed so happy, and I would wonder how she was so happy with all she had to do. My dad also carried a heavy load with working construction all day then working the farm the rest of the time. All this was accomplished without complaining. I remember my very early years as a learning experience on the farm as far as all the wonders of the world God had made and made available to me. I also learned much from two older brothers as far as hunting and fishing, and I also began to learn the tricks boys pull on each other. This remains with me even today.

My grandparents played a huge role in my upbringing, for they instilled in me the same work ethic that my parents had shown me. It was also during these times that I was exposed to five wonderful aunts and uncles. Strangely enough, there were three aunts and uncles on both my dad's side of the family as well as on my mother's side of the family and one special great-uncle on my dad's side that helped to mold me into the man I am today. These aunts and uncles shared the same beliefs in God taught to me by my parents, and these beliefs meant so much to me. These aunts and uncle would produce twenty-three wonderful cousins my brothers and I would grow up with together. We would experience a wonderful childhood together. This support carried me through many of the bipolar episodes I probably experienced in my early childhood years. Again, I or my parents did not think anything of the behavior I displayed, for I had few periods of depression to go along with the manic episodes. I felt I was normal in the sense that I acted like any other child of my age. I can remember all those family reunions held at various parks and all those Christmas parties that had a carnival atmosphere that helped to make up pleasant childhood memories. One particular uncle gave me my sense of humor during these times, for he would always be quick with a trick or joke that made me laugh to the point I found myself wanting to pull stunts on him.

One particular Christmas, I remember putting an electric cord in the end of a corncob for his present from me. Another time I wrapped a cow pie in a cake box, wrapped it, and put it under the tree. It was these times that added that special flavor in my life that are so dear to me, that will forever be etched in my very soul. These simple times with family and on the farm made me realize how important the good times in life were to me, and they planted a strong commitment to family that I desire today.

It was also during these days on the farm that I noticed, as I arose early each morning to work on the farm, how important it was for me to witness the rising of the sun and how I felt this special closeness with nature and God as I saw the sun crack the eastern sky. I never realized then that this seemingly insignificant event would be a very important part of my day, for I felt God's presence each time I saw it come up. These times on the farm also taught me a strong work ethic taught to me by my mother and father: if you did not work, you did not eat. Sometimes these values were taught to me on the end of a belt or a willow switch. These are the lessons one never forgets. These were special times for me, and they remain with me always. It would not dawn on me till some years later how important it was for me to understand the significance of these times early in my life.

Soon it was time to go to school, and I would be away from home for really the first time with the exception of a few times I spent at my grandparents' home. It was during these short trips away at my grandparents' that I learned more values I could apply to my life. I was lucky in the sense that both sets of grandparents were Christian people, and their values were the same as the ones I had been taught at home. I at times got into trouble at their homes and would receive some form of punishment there as well; I always deserved what I got. I remember one time in particular at my Grandma Morris's home. I had arrived there in my Sunday clothes, and she had told me not to get my clothes dirty, for they were my Sunday clothes. As I wandered around this wonderful farm, I noticed a small turtle in Grandpa's pond. I collected these paint turtles, as they called them. I knew I had to have it, so I put a board out into the pond so I could walk out on it then catch this turtle. As I reached to get the turtle, I lost my balance and fell face-first into this nasty pond. I had no choice but to head to the house and tell Grandma what had happened. She said nothing as I went to the back door, only to go to the smokehouse and get a number 10 washtub and meet her in the backyard. Down in the lot, Grandpa was talking some business with some other men. Grandma directed me to put some water in the tub, which was located on a long table in the backyard she used for canning. As I stood there, she instructed me to take off all my clothes and get into the tub. I told her all the men could see me, but she insisted I remove my clothes anyway. As I sat down in that tub, I remember to this day how embarrassed I was as those men laughed at me. I can tell you one thing, that I never doubted Grandma when she told me not to do something again.

Many other stories come to mind when I think of the many adventures to my grandparents' homes, stories I will cherish forever for these two sets of grandparents helped mold me into what I am today. Another special learning experience came when I started school. For me this was a chance to be around other kids and play and have fun, but some of the classes bored me a lot. Again I learned some new tricks that I could have fun with, so I added them to my arsenal. I was an average student most of my school years. If the subject interested me, I would do good, but if not, I was only average. When I was eight years old, something happened to me that would change my life forever. While at a revival meeting at a Southern Baptist Church near my hometown of Crab Orchard, I sat listening to the preacher talk about salvation and burning in hell and how one could save themselves from eternal damnation and about the steps one must take to ensure going to heaven. It was there that night that I gave my life to the Lord and began my Christian walk with the Lord. This would turn out to be the most important thing in my life, and it launched me on a very wonderful journey. This journey would take me to some very wonderful places in this world and open my eyes to the many wonders God has intended for us to enjoy. Along these paths, I would meet some of the most interesting people who have influenced my life and have added that special spice that have helped to shape me into the person I am today.

When I was nine years old, something happened to me that built in me a deep passion that remains with me even today. It was a Saturday in the spring. My dad was preparing the field in front of my present-day home for that year's crops. I was bringing him a jug of water, when I looked down on the ground and saw this strange rock, one like I had never seen before. It was made of flint and appeared like a Christmas tree. It was an arrowhead, and suddenly I had my first hobby. I began a collection that day that consumed many hours of my time. It was then that a deep passion was formed, for as I began to study the Indian culture, I finally understood that my hands were the first human hands to touch these artifacts in thousands of years. I would hunt many places and find many arrowheads and hatchets, but I would always seem to come back to this one place on my father's farm, for it was special to me because it was here where my quest began when I was only nine years old.

I cannot imagine how many hours of my life have been devoted to this simple hobby. Each trip is different from the rest as I search for these artifacts from this ancient past. I can remember times when I could not wait for the fields to be tilled and for good rain to come.

SUNRISE

It was then that I would put on my boots and walk the fields to find these seemingly insignificant rocks. I can remember one day I found twenty-five whole arrowheads and how my pockets were bulging when I went home that afternoon. I have hunted arrowheads my entire life and now have a four-hundred-piece collection that I am very proud of. I have never sold one, nor have I bought one. I have found them all. My wife and I have three beautiful daughters. I have taught them this simple hobby over the years. I now have a wonderful grandson, and I cannot wait for the day I can take him by the finger and lead him into these fields and show him the secrets of our ancient past.

Telling this brings to mind another story that happened some forty years later, which still stirs a deep passion in me. It was early June. My father had tilled these same fields and was waiting for the rains that would moisten these fertile fields before the planting. It was 4:30 a.m. I could hear the distant thunder from the west that was soon replaced with the gentle pecks of rain that was soon replaced with sheets of rain that pelted the back of the house I had built. I stirred around in the darkness and gathered my clothes, being careful not to wake my wife. I passed up the hallway, and I saw that my daughter was fast asleep. I went into the kitchen, grabbed a bite, and stepped out and took my first breath of the new day. The rains soon subsided; it was then that I gazed to the east and noticed how dark the soil looked on the ridges of the field I always hunted. I went to the barn and started my four-wheeler and made that mere quarter-mile trip to the land of an ancient past. As I entered the field, I could see chips of flint that lay on the ground. It was not long till I saw the tip of an arrowhead protruding from the ground. It was a small St. Charles dovetail, and suddenly the lack of sleep and the mud I encountered were all worthwhile. That day I found eight complete arrowheads and the tip of a hatchet. At that point, I closed my eyes and took a trip I have taken many times in the forty-plus years I have roamed these lands. I closed my eyes and stepped back into the past. In my vision, I could smell the campfires and could see a woman cooking over a fire, and I could see children running wildly with bows and arrows and playing without fear. I could hear in the distance the sound of a man chipping flint to make the arrowheads he would use to kill game or to protect his family. My eyes shifted to the creek nearby. I noticed how clear it was. Absent were garbage or chemicals. You could see the fish swimming; it was so clear. My eyes soon shifted to the west. Absent were roads and power lines or the vapor trails of airplanes. In the fields, there were no tractors that tilled the fields. Around me were only green forests and gentle plains and quiet people that took care of the land, and the land in turn took care of them. I wondered what these people were like and where they came from and what caused them to leave. I will never have answers to these questions, but I feel the coming of the white man influenced this greatly. As I opened my eyes, my journey came to an end.

Over the years, I have taken this journey countless times. I have walked hundreds of miles in these fields in quest of my passion. I have never left unsatisfied. Someday I hope my grandchildren will take me by the finger and let me lead them into these passionate places of our ancient past. Today, each time I walk these fields, I would feel this same thrill and closeness to God and nature and this same connected feeling with these ancient Indian ancestors. As the spring comes and the fields are tilled up and the rains have come, I feel as though I am that small boy that waits for that first rain as I did over forty years ago. Things like these are ingrained in us all for they are the things that make us who we are. My parents ingrained in me the importance of a relationship with Jesus Christ, and it has stayed with me my entire life, for you see, as I enter these fields even today, I not only experience the passion for arrowhead hunting, but I also experience God and all he has made.

There are so many stories that I have that center on the farm, and it is funny how they are pulled up from my memory. As one is told, another seems to appear. Sometimes we only have to push our recall button to make these stories live again. This brings to mind another story of my years on the farm. One day when I was eleven years old, my mother told me to go get my next oldest brother for dinner. He was two years older than me, and we were just getting to the stage where we wanted to cuss a bit. He was cleaning off the hog floor and had knee boots on as he waded hog manure. I knew he could not get to me very quick, so I cussed him and told him to get his ass to the house; it was dinnertime. He cussed me back and struggled to get off the floor so he could get to me. I ran, for I knew I could get to the safety of Mom before he could get me. About halfway to the house, a plan of a stunt I could pull on him came to me. I had this hatchet on my belt, which I won for selling seeds this past fall. I got it from my belt and embedded it in a block of wood. I unbuttoned my shirt and set it on my chest and buttoned my shirt back around it. My plan was to make him think the hatchet was stuck in my chest. At that point, I heard a scream, but from the opposite direction. Our mother had come to see what was taking so long. She thought my brother had killed me. I could not get up fast enough, for my mother nearly beat me to death with her fists. My brother sure got a kick out of this. This was one stunt that had backfired on me.

It was in the fifth grade that I began to notice girls, and school suddenly took on a new twist for me. On the farm you were too busy to think about anything as silly as girls, so this was a new adventure for me. It was in the sixth grade that I noticed one girl in particular that seemed to have caught my eye. She was so much different than the rest of the girls, for she cared not if she got muddy or her clothes got dirty, and she was the best softball player of all the girls. She even shared some of the same hobbies I had, such as fishing and arrowhead hunting. On through school we went, and I began to see how smart she was, and she even lived close to me, and boy, how pretty she was. On our eighth-grade trip to St. Louis, I gave this same girl my identification bracelet, and suddenly I had my first girlfriend. She would end up being the only girl I would ever date. It was during these years I that became a Boy Scout. My scout leader became one of my most important role models. He instilled in me not only the scouts' honor but also the Christian values I live by today. His teachings have played a huge role in my life, and they can never be replaced. The many meetings and camping trips he took us on are among the many valued lessons he taught me in life and are among my fondest memories of my early years. Mr. O. was always there to lead me. My high school years were much like my grade school years, for I was a C average student. I liked to laugh a lot. This sometimes got me into trouble. Again, as before, I was adding more ammunition to my arsenal. My high school years were fun for me for I had no pressure on me and cannot remember any bipolar episodes for there was very little stress. If there were any periods of the disorder, I would not have noticed them, for I had no idea I was bipolar at that time.

I worked on the farm and did custom hay baling during the summer. These times were really fun for me. All my life I have hunted mainly rabbit and quail around this region. I enjoyed hearing the dogs run a rabbit or point that quail, and I would kill the game and eat it. This desire to kill game would end one hot August in 1969. I had gone up to my uncle's farm to help take up hay. As I arrived that day, my cousin showed me this small deer he had caught in the hay field. It was a tiny doe with fresh white spots. I joked and told my aunt that it was what I wanted for pay instead of money. I remained at their home for one week while the hay was put up, and to my surprise, when I got ready to leave, there was that same deer complete with a halter leash, awaiting me. After getting her home, I put her in the basement while I changed my clothes. When I went to the basement, there was my younger brother with the deer. What shocked me was that he was feeding the deer brine pickles from a large crock my mother had put down prior to canning. I do not know how many of the pickles the deer had eaten, but she ate them like candy. I made a pen for the deer. I named her Baby, but I could not hold her because of her jumping ability, so I let her run free. She knew where her bottle came from, so each time she was hungry, she would come and paw on the back door. This delighted my mother a lot, for while I was at school, she was the chief deer feeder. After raising this deer, I saw how smart she was and decided at that point I could never kill one of the wonderful animals again. Soon Baby got much bigger, and she began to wander more and more, and it became time for her to think of having her own fawn someday.

One day I was at the neighbor's house, baling hay, and she came into the field and asked me what that was in the field. I looked and saw a deer standing with the cattle and wondered if by chance it could be Baby. In the past, I had always whistled and called her by name, so I did that day. To my amazement, she came running toward me and threw that keen nose in the air and came up to me. I fed her a stick of chewing gum and petted her awhile, and she finally drifted off that day. This would be the last time I would see Baby. This was a wonderful experience with wildlife and how God had exposed me to the many wonders he has bestowed us on this earth. The years in school seemed like the most boring years at that time to me, but as I got older, I now know these were the wonderful times. Absent were worry and the pressures of making a living, paying taxes, and all the other things that go with being an adult.

As I left school and entered the navy, I stepped into a totally different world. Soon it was off to boot camp for me and separation from the ones I loved. This same girl would also move away to a nursing school in St. Louis. This would be the first time I had been away from home or this same beautiful girl I was in school with. Boot camp was a culture shock for me. Not only had I never been yelled or abused but I also had never been around any other ethnic groups other than my own. I soon adapted to the yelling and screaming, as well as the other ethnic groups. Eight weeks is a long time to be away from someone if you have never experienced it before. You really have some time to focus on your family and realize the things they have told you are true and that they are not as stupid as you thought they were. Soon I would be home for my first leave since enlisting, and I would spend Christmas with my family. During these same times, this same girl and I would look at engagement rings at a local jewelry store, and she would tell of a ring she thought was pretty. Little did she know that I would go back and put money down so I could mail money home and pay for it while I was away in Pennsylvania. It was after this leave I would fly to Philadelphia, Pennsylvania, for the first schools. These schools would teach me firefighting skills as well as NBC warfare.

While in Philadelphia, I had the chance of a lifetime as I ventured to Independence Hall and, for the first time, heard Walter Cronkite narrate the history of the Liberty Bell. This sent chills up my spine as I stood in front of the Liberty Bell and viewed the large crack in it. I also got to view the first Continental Congress as it appeared in the 1870s, and I felt how these meetings had shaped the beginnings of our great country. Many hours of my weekends were spent here as I enjoyed the history that surrounded me. Also close to Independence Hall was a wax museum where many of history's most prominent people were displayed. Some of the figures could move and even talk by tape as you stood there in amazement. A strange thing happened to me as I stood there, for I began to think how much we are all like these wax figures. We want to appear on the surface to be someone we are not, for no one knows what is inside us, and these figures can talk and say the things we all want to hear, much like us. How many times have I simply said what a person wants to hear to gain favor or to get my way?

After these schools were completed, I went home again and gave this same girl an engagement ring around Christmas. As we sat in my dad's old '67 Chevy on the square in our hometown, I gave her this same ring. She cried and slipped it on her finger and could not wait to show it to her parents. I still remember the glow on her face. After this leave, I flew to San Diego, California, to attend welding school. This flight was a strange experience for me, for I flew out of St. Louis in dress blues and a heavy pea coat, only to lay over in Arizona and step into eighty-degree weather. Then finally on to California. This was a new world for me to bask in the warm sun of California, much different than the snow

Hot Dogger

we had back home. While there I got to surf in the warm Pacific Ocean and see how much different the people seemed; they were not as friendly as the folks of Southern Illinois. They were just too busy to take the time for a person like I was used to. While there I had the chance to venture outside the border of the United States for the first time. You can cross the border into Mexico to Tijuana and enter a new world. As I crossed that bridge into Mexico, I saw poverty for

SUNRISE

the first time and felt ashamed of how much I enjoyed and how little these graceful people seemed to have. Below that bridge I saw people living in cardboard houses, and some of the children ran around without clothes and begged for money as we passed. I wondered how this could be that our countries were this close and yet so far apart. I could not understand how they seemed so happy with their lot in life and how miserable people in the States seemed, at times so ungrateful with all they had. There are so many beautiful sights and history in Mexico to be shared by all, and I was honored to be a part of it. Of the many trips I made into this city, I would always be careful not to let the sun set on me in Mexico, for I had heard all the horror stories of sailors locked up in a Mexican jail for petty crimes. I never spent one minute after dark there.

As I worked to complete my welding school, I found myself pushing myself to do well. I enjoyed making things with my hands and welding things together. This gave me a sense of accomplishment. I graduated in the upper 10 percent of my class, so I got a better choice on my new duty station and my ship. I had finally found my niche in life in welding and felt I was destined to become a welder. Soon it was time to graduate from welding school and be home again prior to moving on to another duty station. In May 1972, I flew into St. Louis, where my girlfriend was attending nursing school. It was a Friday, the day I always called her. I was in my dress whites and was tanned from the warm California sun. I went to the parking lot by her dormitory and called the pay phone that was on her floor; the number was 314-721-9544, a number I will never forget. Someone else answered the phone and went to get her. As she answered the phone, we chatted for a minute, and I asked her what the weather was like there. She answered she was not sure. I then asked her to step to the window of her fourth-floor dormitory and look outside and tell me what the weather was. As she pulled back the curtain and looked out, I stepped from the phone booth and waved to her. She was so shook up her roommate had to dress her. This was one of my most favorite stunts I have pulled over the years.

My orders finally came in. I was to fly to Charleston, South Carolina, and was assigned to the Destroyer Escort USS *Brumby*

DE1044. Upon arrival in Charleston, my ship was not there; it was in Cuba, so I had to wait one week to join my ship. These times were particularly hard for me, for I was put on another ship until they flew me to Cuba. These were the times I felt alone and thought at times I was losing my mind. I was sick much of the time and threw up many times. As I think back, I feel this was really my first episode into a bipolar world, for the depression consumed me to the point I could not function or think clearly. Everything around me seemed fuzzy, and I felt worthless and began to second-guess myself. Finally, the time came for me to fly to Cuba and catch up with *Brumby*. As we flew toward Cuba, I noticed how the plane would veer as we flew along the coast of Cuba, and I asked one of the attendants if there was some sort of trouble with the plane. She informed me we had to adjust our course to avoid Communist air space to not cause us to be shot down.

The first three days on *Brumby* were very rough, for not many people spoke to me, and again I felt all alone. Again I felt these were the deep part of the bipolar depression I had experienced while in Charleston, and it followed me to Cuba. Finally one day, as I lay in our berthing space, this huge man from Texas seemed to see how bad I felt and leaned down and stuck out his huge right hand and said, "They call me Hot-Dogger." Suddenly my fears began to melt, and I felt like one of the boys at last. We formed a friendship that day that would last our entire time in the navy, and that friendship is still intact to this day. Of all the places our ship went, our friendship would carry me on with a closeness only felt by true friends. I feel we all have a Hot-Dogger in our lives to pull us up when we are down. We only have to take the time to recognize them.

Finally, it was back to Charleston, and I finally began my life on board ship. I remember my early days in the repair shop with a group of men I would grow to be close to. It was there I worked for one of the meanest men I have ever met. He was the type of man that cursed you and threatened you if you did not complete the assigned task he had given you to do. It was then I vowed that if I ever got the chance to run that shop, I would never treat anyone this way. As I worked in the shop and began to know the men that worked there, I started to understand the workings of a navy ship and see how important it was to work as a unit. I soon took advancement tests and began to advance in my rate, and along with this came more responsibility and more headaches. Soon some of the older guys started to be discharged, and some of us younger ones began to step up into their shoes. Finally, the one guy that gave us so much trouble was gone, and we finally had a shop we could work in harmony. We began to prepare for a cruise that would take us away from home for three to four months. This would be my first trip at sea, and I was somewhat concerned about it. As the cruise approached, I would make weekend trips to St. Louis to see my girlfriend. This helped to calm the fears of being away from home somewhat. This cruise would give us the opportunity to test the training we had received in our schools and also give us some experience at sea. I remember that first day at sea like it was yesterday, and I remember what they fed us at the noon meal. We were served greasy spare ribs that would end up making us sick as the ship rocked back and forth. I also remember how they laughed at us as we threw up over the side. This would be the only time I would be sick the rest of the time I was in the navy.

Soon we found ourselves on this NATO cruise that would send us deep into the North Atlantic to run with ships of various nations and test our systems and ordinance. One day while on maneuvers, our boilers failed. We were adrift without propulsion in the choppy North Atlantic. They soon towed us up the Firth of Clyde into Faslane, Scotland. We remained there for three months while they decided what to do with us. Scotland is a beautiful country with people that make you feel welcome; we felt at home there. Many meals of fish and chips were eaten there, and the hospitality these people showed will never be forgotten. One day Hot-Dogger came to the shop and asked me if I had any old welding rods he could have, and I directed him to a fifty-pound box that had gotten wet and could no longer be used. I asked him what he needed them for, and he told me it was none of my business and left. For the next three evenings after work, he would come to the shop and sharpen the rods to a fine point, and I would ask him what he was doing, with the same response. Finally one day he asked me to get a loaf of bread and meet him on top to the hangar bay. I did as he said and watched him climb the ladder that led to the top of the hangar bay. I again asked him what he was doing. He replied, "You'll see." It was then that he told me to start throwing the bread into the air, and I figured out his plan. For as I threw the bread into the air, the seagulls would swoop down to catch it, and he would throw the welding rods at them. He had spent three days preparing these weapons, and it took him less than three minutes to throw them without a single kill. Again he had made me laugh and helped me through these times.

Me at sea

Finally the word came that we were to either be towed across the rough North Atlantic or go to the shipyards in South Hampton, England. Finally word came down that we would be towed across the Atlantic to our homeport in Charleston, South Carolina. They had told us that married men and nonessential personnel would go back to the States via another ship, so it was no surprise to me when I received word that I would be left on *Brumby*. By this time, I had advanced quickly and become the senior hull technician (HT) on board. I also was in charge of the repair parties and taught firefighting and damage control on board. I had been assigned to run the repair shop and had eight men working for me. I learned quickly to ask my men to do a job, never to tell them, for these men would jump off that ship if I asked them to. To me they were among some of the finest men on board *Brumby*. We got along so well and laughed a lot every day as we did our repairs and became so close, a closeness one must have if you are to survive at sea. Our relationship was envied by the other divisions on board, and some wanted to join our elite group. Even after a day working at sea, we still would hang around each other and enjoy our time off.

At last the tug came for us, and we set out on our trip across these rough waters. It was during these dark times that I found myself

SUNRISE

awake long before daylight, for this was my time when all was quiet. There was no noise except the sound of the ocean. One morning I got up before daylight and went topside and went to the bow of this huge ship. I went in front of the gun mount and found myself staring as the glow of the presun lit that eastern sky. It was then I remembered that special feeling of the closeness I had felt as a young man as I anticipated God's arrival, for I had forgotten these feelings in the fast-paced and busy life I had. A chill went over me as the sun cracked that calm ocean, and to me the face of God was cast on that tranquil sea. Suddenly all my fears began to fade, and the problems I thought I had faded away. I experienced many sunrises while at sea, one just as spellbinding as the other, and each time God was there with me. In turn, I would be on the fantail in the evening to witness the setting of the sun. You see, the setting and rising of the sun bears a different meaning to me than most. The setting of the sun signifies the death of Christ, when all the earth turned dark and despair filled the land. In turn, the rising of the sun to me is the resurrection of Christ as he comes as he promised to bring light to the dark of this world. As the light of the sun came up, I could see so many beautiful things God has bestowed upon us all in the world we live in and how blessed we all are. These times at sea and the rising of the sun took me back to the days of my childhood on the farm, where my first experience of the rising sun occurred. The excitement I felt was the same, and I was now as then in amazement of this simple yet essential part of my day.

On the Bow

After one week at sea, a weather report came that we could be in the path of a typhoon, but they felt we would be safe. By 4:00 p.m., it was very apparent they had been wrong. The seas began to get rough, and all watertight doors were ordered closed. The tug struggled to keep us into the waves as it pulled us at four knots. At 5:00 p.m. no one was to be above the main deck; the seas were getting rougher. I was assigned the midwatch that night, which meant I would stand watch from 12:00 midnight to 4:00 a.m. I had decided to get some sleep before my watch, so I went to bed around 7:00 p.m. By 8:00 p.m. I had been thrown from my rack four times. I finally got up and went to the log room to check the clinometers; this instrument tells how much of a roll the ship is taking. By this time, the ship was taking forty- to forty-five-degree rolls. Even walking inside the ship was hard. At midnight I assumed the watch. This watch is called sound and security watch, which consists of carrying a .45-caliber pistol and a sounding tape. This tape is to be put down tubes that run to the bottom of the ship to check for leaks. At 2:00 a.m. I went to report the ship was secure. As I entered the bridge where they steered the ship from, a huge black man who was at the helm told me the tow had broken. It then occurred to me we were severed from the tug. There we were in thirty-five-foot seas with no power in the middle of a typhoon. I remember thinking of home and my parents and girlfriend and thought I would never see them again. It was then I remember of the ship and caught a light way off to the left. It was the light on the stern of the tug, and suddenly despair was replaced with hope; this feeling I will never forget. None of us slept the rest of the night, but as the sun rose the next morning from a wonderfully calm ocean, our fears began to subside. This sight again reminded me that God was in control. We were attached to the tug and continued on our journey home.

  This really had no bearing on me at that time. It was simply another page in my past. It would not become clear until years later when our middle daughter was having some trouble in college. She had been accepted to St. Louis University in St. Louis to attend occupational therapy school. While home one weekend, her boyfriend called me and told me she was having trouble going back after the weekend. I went to her and talked for over two hours and told her she needed to be sure this school was what she wanted. She was concerned that if she chose not to go back, her mother and I would be mad at her, for we had invested much money into this school. I told her the only thing I was worried was her happiness. I went on to tell her she was simply in a storm much like the storm I had encountered in the North Atlantic, and I shared with her the story you have just read. I told her sometimes it storms in our lives till we think it will never end, and we fear things will never work out or be normal as they were. The storms of life are much like the storms of the sea, for they are usually short-lived and the sun always comes up the next morning. She chose not to go back and continued her education in counseling, and recently she attained her master's degree. Through all these times, I had few times of depression, although as I think back, I guess I experienced several periods of mania. The depression I felt was the times I felt so alone and had fears I would never see my loved ones again, but they were short-lived because of the support of my shipmates. To me, I was feeling normal feelings that we all felt because of being thousands of miles away from home. I had no idea I was bipolar at that time.

As we continued the remainder of our cruise on the rope of that tug, we were put in dry dock in Charleston to have extensive repairs done to our boilers. We stayed in dry dock for eight months till we were again set afloat on the Cooper-Santee River, on our way back to the piers of Charleston. On April 28, 1973, I married the same girl I gave an identification bracelet to in the eighth grade, and life became somewhat complicated, but in a pleasant way. Soon I

At Sea Refueling

was off on another cruise, but this time it would be on a six-month cruise to the Mid East. In November of 1973, we left; this would be the longest separation from my new wife and my family I had ever experienced. I remember now that I hit a depression that was again part of my bipolar disorder that I had no idea I had. Several weeks passed, and at last we hit the west coast of Africa at Dakar, Senegal.

Again I experienced culture shock, for these people were much different than any people I had ever seen. Dakar is a city of five hundred thousand people. It dates back to Henry the Navigator in the fifteenth century, the home to twenty-five thousand Europeans and eight thousand Lebanese, as well as the remainder Africans. Our next stop on our journey led us to Freetown, Sierra Leone, a small country on the hump of Africa. This city gained fame during the times of Napoleonic era as the first home for returning slaves in Africa. Travel for the crew was mainly by bicycle, and I was no different, for I had built a massive bicycle rack in the hangar bay to house many bicycles for our trip to Africa. It was there I tasted my first of many wonderful foods of the African people. I had met a couple from the Peace Corps that had invited me to join them in the jungle for an evening meal. I was to bring nothing, only me along with some of the other crew members. They prepared this meal in a huge kettle for all to enjoy. As I watched the meal being prepared, I remembered the Tarzan movies I had watched as a kid and how they had cooked people in these kettles. I looked around, and all I could see were Africans. What a laugh I got out of this for thinking this way.

We set sail from this wonderful place and experienced something that will remain with me forever. This was the crossing of the equator. When a person crosses this for the first time, navy tradition states you will have a ceremony to remember this crossing. It consist of crawling through these troughs of leftover food of the previous two days and being beaten with sections of fire hose, not hard, but enough to get your attention. You then have to crawl up to King Neptune and kiss his belly. These ceremonies are conducted by officers and enlisted men who have already crossed the equator. It is a fun day for all, and after completing this, you are considered a shellback. Soon it was around the Cape of South Africa and on to Port Louis, Mauritius. On Christmas Eve after a twenty-one-day 6,200-mile leg of our journey, we tied to the pier at Port Louis. Port Louis is a city of eight hundred thousand people comprised of five hundred thousand Indians, twenty-thousand Chinese, and ten thousand Europeans, with the remainder being Africans. Port Louis was no doubt the best shopping stop thus far on our trip. It was here I spent my first Christmas ever away from home, and I still remember how depressed I was. I stayed this way for three days until again Hot-Dogger and the rest of the crew snapped me out of the grasp of my bipolar skid. With the fast pace of a cruise like this, I could now see I would not notice a manic episode at all, for I had to maintain this pace to keep up with the excitement of running a repair shop and keeping up with all the repairs that go along with keeping a ship running smoothly and being responsible for the well-being of eight other sailors in my charge. Along with being in charge of damage control and firefighting schools came this same breakneck speed I had to maintain. Again I seemed normal to myself, but maybe not to those around me. While in Port Louis, we got our first glimpse of Russian ships and the sailors of the largest navy in the world. We were not allowed to converse with them because they were as much in awe as we were.

Our next stop would take us to the Seychelles Islands, a British Crown colony that was a true tropical paradise located in the heart of the Indian Ocean. Victoria is the capital and the largest city of the colony. Only sixty thousand people inhabit the entire island. *Brumby* dropped anchor on the second day of the New Year in Victoria, and we found ourselves entering a paradise. The beauty of the island was captivating to us all. The vegetation, flowers, and coconut palms covered the island, as well as pineapple and vanilla plants to go along with the orange, mange, pear, breadfruit, and mango trees that all added flavor to this area none of us had ever seen. This was by far the cleanest, most pristine port we had visited. The last day on Victoria, a huge beach party was held for the entire crew. Seven hundred hotdogs, along with eighty pounds of hamburger, were consumed along with thirty cases of American beer, the first we had on our journey to the Mid East. As we left and skirted up the rugged coastline, we encountered a large anchorage of Russian ship in an inlet. There were nuclear submarines as well as huge cruisers and fast attack vessels that dwarfed *Brumby*. After the cruisers trained their guns on us, we decided it was not the place for us, so we retreated to the safety of the sea.

On we steamed toward our next port of call, Karachi, Pakistan. Our six-day visit to Karachi would be the highlight of our cruise, for there was some of the best shopping there of all the ports. Whether one needed wooden products or the vast array of brass or anything else you could imagine, Karachi was the place. One could spend days browsing in the various shops that included brass, wood, and silk or tapestries like none I had ever seen. Sightseeing was something to behold in Karachi. The countryside was beautiful, and the people were extremely hospitable. It was there I had the chance to take my first ever camel ride. I had always heard they had terrible breath and body odor. They had told me right. The ride was fun but short for I could not hold my breath very long. It was in Karachi that I first encountered the Muslim religion. One day I was walking in the city, when all of a sudden everyone stopped and dropped to their knees and faced one direction. I later learned they were facing Mecca and this was their prayer time. I froze and remained silent for I did not want to make anyone mad at me. While in Karachi, I had the opportunity to visit the tomb of a great leader of Pakistan. This tomb was made entirely out of gold and silver. What a sight to behold! This was another culture I was to encounter on my journey.

Our next leg of the journey would take us to Bandar Abbas, Iran. Located in the Straits of Hormuz, this town would be our first experience with Persian expansion. It was during this time that something happened to me that terrified me. One night as I sat writing my new wife a letter, I heard someone coming into the shop. As I looked up, I saw one of the guys that worked for me enter the door. He was standing watch and waving a .45-caliber pistol in the air. He stated he was going to kill them. I asked him who, and he told me the guys that had come back to the ship from Kharg Island, Iran. As I saw the gun had a full clip in, I started for the door. He pointed the gun at my head and just stood there. For seconds that seemed like hours, our eyes stared at each other. I knew I had to do something, so I asked him what gun he held, that it looked like the gun I had used the previous day. I told him the gun had jammed on me and needed repair. To my astonishment, he handed me the gun, which I immediately cleared. He then gave me the extra clip and began to cry. I told him to get a cup of coffee while I checked the weapon. I ran as fast as I could to my division officer's berthing space to tell him of what had happened. He immediately sent a detail to the shop and put this man in a straitjacket. He was lifted by helicopter that morning to be evaluated for a nervous breakdown.

After a short one-day visit there, we were off to Bandar Shahpur, which offered little to do. Sixty of the crew had the opportunity to go on a great visit to Persepolis, a 2500 Bc city that had been excavated from the desert. The then in power shah sent a personal airplane down to transport this group of sixty. I was fortunate enough to make this trip, for I am very interested in archeology. The shah had personally approved this visit. To me this was the highlight of the entire cruise. Soon we were at sea again, headed for Bahrain Island, which is nestled in the Persian Gulf. This area, which offered our first taste of American culture, was well welcomed to us all. As I reflected on the places and people we had encountered, I could see God's hand in them all and stood in wonder of all he had created. I still would arise each morning to witness the sunrise that cast its eye over these wonderful places. Soon we were on to Djibouti in the territory of French Afars, an arid desert at the western end of the Gulf of Aden, close to Addis Ababa, the capital city of Ethiopia to the west. This port was very expensive as we got a taste of the culture there. As I viewed the people of this region, I felt somewhat ashamed of all that we had back in the States, for these people had little as far as material things went but seemed so content with their lot in life. Seeing so many cultures and religious beliefs yet only one God had created them all left me spellbound. It was at this port where we turned around and began to retrace our steps back to the south and down the eastern coast of Africa. It sure felt good for us all to know we were on the downhill side of this long cruise.

After many days at sea, we tied to the pier in Mombasa, Kenya. This was also a highlight for all of *Brumby*, for this was the port where we would meet with the USS *Paul*, which was our relief ship. While in Kenya, seventy of the crew were selected to go to the largest wildlife reserve in the world. I was fortunate enough to be among this group. We took a 250-mile trip into the interior of Kenya in Land Rovers, which was quite tiring. On this trip we had the opportunity to see oryx, elands, giraffes, gazelles, rhinos, elephants, zebras, and baboons.

This is one trip I will never forget. I could not see these sights without thinking again of all that God had created, for these places on this great plain were so beautiful and serene. Absent were all the material things we think are so vital in our lives. As we arrived back in Mombasa, I was snapped back into reality; my adventure was over.

One day while we were tied to the pier, some natives came alongside in dugout boats, selling various items, from produce to carved items. Hot-Dogger and I were on the starboard side, watching them. Some dove for money as they watched us. He asked me for my keys to the repair shop, and I asked him why. He at that point told me it was none of my business and again asked for the keys. He soon returned with a double handful of small washers. He knew that the natives would think the washers were money, and he winked at me. As he yelled and threw the washer over the side, the natives dove after them as he laughed. They soon surfaced, and I know they cussed him in their native tongue. What a laugh we all had that day.

Soon we would be in our dress whites and assembled on the deck of *Brumby*. Navy tradition says you will ring the entire deck of the ship as you turn over command to another ship when they relieve you. Finally, after a long extended cruise, it was time for us to turn over command to the USS *Paul* DE-1080. As we backed out the harbor in Mombasa the ninth of April, someone slipped a Simon & Garfunkel tape into the ship's system, and the song "Homeward Bound" suddenly embraced us all. That song to this day fills me with emotion. For we were finally bound for home after all those long weeks at sea. It also speaks to me in my present life, that I long to be homeward bound to heaven to be with God and my loved one who have passed on before me. I knew we, on that great ship, had run a good race and cruised a good cruise, and it was time to go home. What a great feeling this was to all those homesick sailors. I can only hope I can run a good race and someday be headed home, for this should be our ultimate goal in life as we cycle through this world we live in.

Our next leg toward home led us to Lourenco Marques, Mozambique. This port turned out to be one of the best ports visited. The beaches were long and clean, and the people were very hospitable. While there, I had the opportunity to witness a bull fight.

SUNRISE

It was much different than most, for in this fight, they did not kill the bull. A mounted horseman would entice the bull to charge him and wear down the bull with repeated lunges. After the bull seemed worn down came a line of Portuguese men that would line up and tackle the bull into submission. After rounding the Cape of South Africa for the final time, we headed for Luanda, Angola, for a two-day stop and refueling. While there we enjoyed the cuisine of the city, but all had their sights on the coast of North America that lay thousands of miles to the west. On farther we would travel up the western coast of Africa to Monrovia, Liberia. This capital city offered its own charm and grace and was enjoyed by all. Liberia was a safe haven for freed US slaves and is the oldest independent country in black Africa. We departed this port and began our long trek across the Atlantic, headed toward South America. This eight-day trip would dock us in Recife, Brazil. While there the members of the crew enjoyed some different kind of liberty from what they had grown accustomed to in Africa. Most had trouble understanding the Portuguese language but could always make them understand the dollar. It was in this port the deckhands began painting the ship to make preparations for our return home. No one complained about this job. Soon we would round the hump of Brazil and head for Port of Spain, Trinidad, and take on fuel for our trip to Puerto Rico and take on some dignitaries and finally start on our last leg toward Charleston, South Carolina. As we steamed silently up the coastline of a continent we longed to see, I again got up in the darkness and again experienced the rising of the sun, and I thanked God for our long journey that had taken us so far. It was then I wondered how one could not see God as the sun rose and exposed all he had created. Sometimes we are blind as far as what we view as important to us, and our vision is obscured to the point that we become blind to the world we live in.

On May 18, 1974, *Brumby* steamed up the Cooper-Santee River into the harbor to the piers in Charleston. What a wonderful sight to see as the crowds filled the pier with flags waving and people cheering as the ship pulled up to be docked. I could see my new wife as she waved to me, and I remember how emotional I got as I stood there on that deck. It has been thirty-three years since that day, and as I sit here writing this, I find tears in my eyes. Of all the ports and many countries we visited, this port was the best, for this was where my heart was with this woman I would spend my life with, the one who would bear my children and make my life complete. We would live together for the first time since being married and start our first home there in Charleston. We would begin our lives together at 6959 South Kenwood in North Charleston, in a tiny one-bedroom apartment that was made into a home by wife, for she added that special touch that only she possessed. We then would meet many other military families that were not only navy but also air force and soon had our own little group to converse with. It was during this time that my wife's brother would come down to spend some time with us. He had never really traveled, so this was a treat for him as well as us.

Soon we would have a new addition to our family in the form of a five-week-old Chesapeake Lab pup by the name of Bullet, and suddenly we had one more mouth to feed as he grew and would give me many fun-filled afternoons when I came home from the ship. Soon our ship would make a two-week trip to Newport, Rhode Island. I had left a wonderful wife and a small pup, only to return to find that same wife and a pup that had grown so much. I wondered if he was the same dog. He had matured, and his legs had gotten much longer. Even his bark had gotten so much deeper that I was amazed. It was during these times that I would take him to an area lake and throw sticks into the water for him to retrieve after getting off work on the ship. These were the good times for us. Absent were the pressures of children and house payments and property taxes that now loom over us all. I think back now we had a perfect life. My time in the navy was getting short. We had begun to think of home and what we would do and where we would live. Soon along came June 7, 1975, and suddenly I was a free man for the first time in four years. We packed up our belongings along with our dog and headed back to God's country, Southern Illinois. Our lives together would begin at 405 East DeYoung Street in Marion, Illinois, in a small two-bedroom trailer. Life would be good there. My wife was a registered nurse and worked at the same hospital I was born in, and I went to college on the GI Bill and took general studies as well as a welding program. This class for me was simple for I had been a welder for four years in the navy. I would go on to be voted the Welder of the Year at John Logan College in 1976. It was this same period of time that we went on vacation to Texas to see one of my navy buddies. I got a phone call that offered me my first real paying job as a welder building the largest dragline in the world. We were very excited about this and finished our vacation in New Orleans and headed home so I could start this new job.

My wife & I

Life again seemed good, but I found myself forgetting about those sunrises of my life that gave my life purpose. It is so easy to forget God when things seem to be going your way. I started this new job in September 1976 and worked there for six months until I received a call from my oldest brother informing me of another job in area coal mine. I told him I was interested in the job, so he set up a date for me to take this welding test. I passed the test and soon was offered this job that paid more money and had better hours and was closer to home. I would remain on this job for over twenty years, and I feel I owe this all to my brother. Our lives were simple then, for money was plentiful and there was not much pressure on us at all. That would all change on March 2, 1977, at 3:55 a.m., when our first daughter was born. She was so beautiful as she nursed my wife and as before her special touch was exposed. This young lady would add so much joy to our lives that we thought we already had, but now we were beginning to experience real joy for the first time. I can remember times as I worked the midnight shift, I would come home to get into bed and have to compete with this wonderful young lady for she had occupied my bed as I worked. I also remember the fun we had as we played and learned together for this was a new experience for us all. As she grew older, she and I were buddies. I wanted to do everything with her, so we were one. Each evening I would take our dog for a walk, and she would accompany us as we would walk around the block. I held the leash in one hand, and her tiny hand would grasp my finger on the other hand. These are times that I hold most precious, and I can close my eyes and relive them.

This young lady would start to grow and soon be in school and start to rise to the top of each of her classes. Whether it was a school class or a church play, she would be one of the best. One Saturday morning, after I had gotten off work, I went to an area pond to fish. It was the end of March and was already warm. I had put two catfish rods out and noticed on the other side of the pond the bass was chasing top-water fish. I picked up my rod and started over there, when I decided I needed an extra spinner bait to take in case I lost one. I decided not to carry my whole tackle box but instead would hook the extra plug in the loose end of my belt. As I arrived, I could see a large wake of the fish, and I cast my rod toward it. That very first cast, the bass hit my line. As I reeled up the slack, I jerked back to set the hook, and it was then that I felt immense pain in my groin area. You see, I had hooked Little Elvis when I set the hook. The bass give up very quickly, and I landed him, threw him back behind me, and began to work on the other plug. After removing the plug, I turned around in amazement to see the largest bass I had ever caught. I got so shook I forgot about the other rods and rushed to my father-in-law's to weigh the fish, which ended up weighing nine pounds. As I took the bass home to show my wife, she wanted to take a picture of it. She then wanted me to hold our new daughter and the bass so she could get a picture of us all. This bass was longer and weighed more than my daughter, but the joy this tiny daughter gave me was much more exciting than any fish could hold. Some days passed till I took this fish to a taxidermist to have it mounted. He asked me what part of Florida I had caught it in, and I replied I had caught it here in Southern Illinois. He then asked me to tell him the fish story behind the catching of this huge fish. I told him the account you have just read, and he was crying with laughter as I told him this story. He asked me why I had worried about the bass more than Little Elvis, and to this I replied, "I knew what I had on that plug was much bigger than what I had on the one on my belt."

Soon we moved from town and lived with her parents while we were constructing a new house on my dad's farm on the ground he had given us. While working on our new home, my wife came to me and informed me that we were expecting our second child. This brought more excitement to us all. It was then I made her quit painting and staining woodwork in our new home for I was in fear of the dangers involved. As spring came, we now were faced with the excitement of not only our daughter but also the arrival of a new baby and the excitement of a new home. On June 24, 1979, at 1:34 p.m., our second daughter arrived. She, to this day, still looks just like my wife, and again as before, my wife's special touch was exposed. This wonderful young lady gave Dad a new outlook on life. She had the ability to light up the entire room with those big eyes, and her smile would melt even the hardest heart. She would be my fishing buddy and arrowhead-hunting buddy, and she was just like her mother in the fact that she cared not if she got muddy and was a good softball player as well. This petite little blonde would grow up to be my boy, not to cut anyone short, but she did all the things a boy would do, so I could see the traits of a boy in her.

Now suddenly our world turned a different way, for we were now in a new home complete with two wonderful daughters. These two girls gave us much joy during these early years, also in the lives of the grandparents, for my wife's parents had no grandchildren, so they worshipped these girls. Our lives seemed very good during these times. We had two of the most wonderful daughters one could ask for. I had a wonderful wife and a good job. It was along about this time I got interested in a new hobby. One day my wife came to me and told me of an old antique table and chairs she had found at a yard sale. She felt if it was refinished, it would look good in our dining room. We went and looked at it and bought it, thus began my love for refinishing old furniture. After three months of hard work, the old table and chairs were finally brought into the warmth of our new home. This table has become the centerpiece of our home and has been the place where my wife and I have made many decisions over the years. This old table also has been the place where many heart-to-heart talks with my three daughters have taken place to discuss the important things that go along with being a teenager—things like curfew, boys, and what kind of car we need to look for. I cannot imagine how many helium balloons this old table has held over the years or how many little girls have sat around this table for the many birthday parties these girls have had. Or how many tears of sadness and joy this old table has absorbed over the years. My most precious memories involve the many meals that have been served at this old table and all the laughter we enjoyed as we fellowshipped with one another. I remember one special Thanksgiving around this old table when both sets of parents were present, as well as our oldest daughter's husband and the other two daughters' boyfriends. But the crowning moment for me was when my mother gave the blessing for the meal, for she was not in good health, and you could barely hear the words she said; this was my Thanksgiving.

As I think of this old table, I wonder what has held it together for all these years. I feel what has held it together has been our family. Sometimes the glue had stretched to the point that it wanted to run and give up and pull apart, but it stayed put and held together. Our family has endured times when it was stretched and pulled apart, but like the old table, it has stayed put and weathered the storms of life. So you see, I view this old table somewhat different than most, for when I look at this old table, I see much more than some wood glued together. I see my family.

A couple of years would pass before I would again encounter another piece of furniture to tackle. I had gone to Herrin, Illinois, to look at an old piano for the girls to play. As I entered the home, the lady showed me the piano and told me of a piece of furniture in the basement I might be interested in. I entered the basement and saw an old pie safe before me, but it was the ugliest piece of furniture I had ever seen. It had been painted in pink and part green; even the tin panels had been painted. I ended up buying the piano, pie safe, and an old school desk for twenty-five dollars and loaded them up in a trailer and headed home. I brought these items home and sat the old pie safe in the garage. It would sit there for nine years, for I could not get enough nerve to tackle this project. Finally one day I decided I would begin this project. I took one section at a time and soon began to see how old this piece was and how beautiful it was as I stripped off the layers of paint. Soon all the stripping was done, and it was glued and stained and varnished. And it was time to move it from the coldness of the garage into the warmth of our home. As my wife and I carried it into our home, she told me how beautiful it was, but I seemed to see something was missing but could not put my finger on it. I left to go to work that day, still not sure of what bothered me so much. All day long I thought of what was missing from the old safe till all of a sudden it was time to go home. As I drove up the driveway that cold December night, I could see my wife had been busy putting up Christmas decorations. As I entered the kitchen, I saw more decorations. It was then that I glanced into the dark dining room and saw the most beautiful sight. I raced to turn on the light, and before me was the old pie safe, only it had been decorated with my wife's special touch, a touch that only she has. This touch has affected me for many years and has been magnified in the lives of our three daughters. Over the years I have finished several pieces of furniture and get satisfaction out of each piece, because in each piece, I see coats of varnish or paint that have covered the beauty that lies beneath. I wonder how many times we discard people we see every day because of the outward appearance or the clothes they wear or the expression on their faces. Many times a beautiful person lies beneath the layers that life has put on these people, if only we will look inside instead of outside.

My job at the coal mines was going very well for me even though much of the time I was depressed and still had no idea I was bipolar. I enjoyed welding for I enjoyed working with my hands and building things, and I took much pride in the work I did. Each day seemed to offer another challenge for me, and I enjoyed these times very much. I had been elected to a position on the safety committee at work, which would add a new dimension to my career in the coal mines. This job consisted of caring for the safety issues of my coworkers as well as the safe running of the mine. As before, I still enjoyed being a prankster and always was quick with a joke or pulling a stunt on my fellow workers. Sometimes these pranks would get me into trouble, but I would do them anyway. I remember one day a gentleman came to me with a ventriloquist dummy he had ordered from a mail order catalog. This man had retired from the mine and thought I would know what to do with this dummy. We had this guy whose lower lip would hang down when he got mad, and we all made fun of him. This dummy also had a lower lip that hung down. As I looked at the dummy, I devised a plan on how I would pull this stunt. I went to the warehouse and told the guy there of the plan I had. He would call this man's foreman and tell him this guy had a package via UPS.

This foreman then took the package down to the pit where this man ran a bulldozer and gave it to him. As he opened the box, he saw this dummy and crammed it back into the box. That afternoon we all kidded him in the bathhouse about this dummy. Some days later, this man told me he was going to Knoxville, Tennessee, on vacation and even told me where he would be staying. This was in 1982, the year of the world's fair. After thinking about it for a while, I devised another plan that would involve calling Knoxville. As I called the motel where he told me he would stay, I asked the person if this man was staying there. He replied yes, and I asked him to connect me with his room. He answered the phone. I posed as the motel manager and asked him for a favor. I then told him our band had canceled for the evening and asked him if he would consider putting on a puppet show. I could feel the heat coming through the phone as he cussed me. He eventually started to laugh and asked me how I knew where he was staying, and to this I replied that he had told me. It was this event and others that would build a friendship that lasts to this day.

The next couple of years went as the previous ones as we raised those wonderful girls in the country and the land that I loved so much. Then as before, I enjoyed the rising of the sun each day and would rise to whatever lay before me. The mines were good to us and allowed us to continue to enjoy a good life. On October 8, 1985, our world took another twist. Our third daughter came into this world at 9:50 p.m. This daughter was perfect as the previous two, and again as before, my wife displayed her special touch that she only possesses. This third daughter grew up with two older sisters and matured quickly. She was much like her older sisters but somewhat different; she was simply herself. She possesses some of the same traits as I do in as much as pulling stunts and having a great sense of humor. She brought so much laughter to our home and could light up the room when she walked in. So now I am totally outnumbered in my own home, but I would not trade my girls for ten boys, for this was what God meant for us to have, or he would not have given them to us. I remember all the laughter and tears that go with raising three girls, for they have brought so much joy to our lives—joy that you cannot buy with all the money this world has to offer.

Nicki, Rene, Author, Amanda, Heather

The Morris family.

SUNRISE

One night I got a phone call from a friend inviting me to coach a girls' softball team at a local country league. After talking awhile, he convinced me to take the job. Suddenly I was the coach of a small team of five- to seven-year-old young ladies. My daughters were part of this team, and after the first game, I was hooked forever as I watched these girls catch that first ball or hit the ball for the first time and score that first run. As I started to enjoy this with great passion, I began to see some improvements that needed to be made to the ball park. I began to call the area merchants and ask for donations to improve this park. One day one of the trustees came to me and said he felt I was trying to take over and said some pretty terrible things to me that made me mad, and I decided to leave the league there. When I left, to my surprise, half the team went with me and moved to a much larger program in the city of Marion. Little did I know how hooked I was as I watched countless young girls turn into young women. I coached all my three girls until they would finally retire from softball and seek other sports and finally boys. The girls and parents thanked me for teaching these girls so much about softball, but I tried to teach them not only about softball but also about life and the joys and also some of the disappointments that go along with it. I tried to teach them that a person will not always win and that losing is also a lesson they must learn because losing will not always be on the ball field; it also happens in life. These same young women now will see me somewhere and come to me and call me coach and hug my neck. This makes those years well worthwhile for me.

I remember one game we had won. All the crowd was gone. I had waited till the last girl was picked up, and I had turned out the lights and loaded my equipment into my truck and lit that cigarette I thought I needed. I had barely got it lit when a small voice came out of the darkness. This voice asked me, "Why do you do that?" As I turned, I saw the dark eyes of a girl that was on the team we had just beaten. I had no answer as I gazed into the eyes of this innocent girl, because I had no defense. This girl lived close to the park and had come to me to see if she could be on my team because we seemed to have so much fun as we played. She had the most beautiful eyes that sparkled and those large dimples as she smiled that could melt the hardest heart. That night there were no dimples, for her eyes demanded answers from a man she thought could do no wrong. I told her that smoking was a terrible habit and I knew I should quit. You see, I was a closet smoker. I thought I could hide this habit, but then I knew I could not hide it from the eyes of a child. This taught me a hard lesson that night, that I might hide from man but I could never hide from God, for he sees all and hears all.

My team that year went on to win our zone tournament and advance on to the nationals in Sterling, Virginia. We competed with teams from around the United States for this coveted title. Our team ended up placing fifth in the nation, not bad for a group on nine- to ten-year-olds. This same girl ended up on my team and got the chance to play in these games with this group of girls. She now is on a scholarship at a Mississippi college playing—you guessed it—softball. These girls taught me much more than I taught her, for she taught me a lesson in life that I will never forget. As I look back to these precious years, I could not tell you how many wins or loses I had, for to me, they were all wins for they taught me that I just wanted to somehow make a difference in the lives of these children. This desire was taught to me by my parents and the extended family as I grew up. I would coach for fifteen years until my daughters would end up losing their desire to play. It was then I retired from coaching. I do not receive a pension for these years of coaching, but I have a wealth of memories that I think of often. These coaching years started my desire of wanting to help children, and it will be rekindled, I am sure, when someday I'll have grandchildren and come out of retirement and again coach. I now have grandchildren of my own and look forward to the day I can live to coach them of the lessons not only in softball but also in life.

On August 19, 1996, the mine closed, and I was unemployed for the first time in my life. I can still remember the pain of being separated from the guys that I had spent more time with over the years than I had spent with my family. You see, I worked seven days a week, even holidays, at work, and suddenly I realized how I had let money separate me from the ones that were most dear to me. I knew their wives' names and even some of the kids' birthdays, for we were a very close-knit group. I was able to give my family all they wanted, but all they wanted was me. Sometimes in life the material things we view as important are really not important at all, for money cannot buy love, for love has no price tag. After losing my job, I drew unemployment. For the first time in twenty years, I felt worthless because I felt as though I was not contributing to the family. I would rock, as they call, it for six months until I was hired at the VA hospital in Marion, Illinois. While there I built the various clinics. As I worked, I met many friends and fit in well with the other workers. One day my boss told me to work at the building I had worked at for several months. That particular day I was tearing out a wall, when I encountered asbestos. I called him on the radio and told him what I had found. Before I could turn around, the place was crawling with people in hazard clothing. My boss was mad at me because I had told of this over the handheld radios we carried. Not long after this incident, I was fired. They gave me no warning or reason, but I know in my mind this incident played a huge role in my dismissal.

So here I am without a job, and I had to go home and face my wife with the news of job loss. Not long after this, they offered me a job as a janitor, which I took, for I had two children in college at that time, so I had to work. This turned out to be the most satisfying job I have ever had, for this gave me the opportunity to visit with the old vets as I cleaned their room. They looked forward to my daily visits, for many had been put there to die. Many seldom had no visitors and felt lonely and were put there simply to die. While working there, I had taken a test for the Department of Corrections and figured I would never hear from them. One night I got home after work, and my wife told me the prison had called to offer me a job. My heart sank for I loved the job I had at the VA. The next day I called the prison, and they offered me a job at the Vienna Correctional Center, which I declined. I told them I did not want to work in a prison. She finally went to tell me I had scored the highest score on the test. Before you think I am so smart, I will tell you the criteria of a prison test. I had done well on the actual test. I also had twenty-plus years work experience, four years navy time, plus I was a supervisor on my ship. Add all this together and you can see what an elevated score I would have. God, in his infinite wisdom, had put all these stumbling blocks in my path simply to get me to this point in my life. Our lives are merely steps. Steps are designed to take us up or down to get us where we need to go in life. I view steps quite differently. I view steps as merely put there to slow me down. The story you are reading of my life is a testimony of a story of the many steps I have taken in my life that taught me God put those steps there for a purpose, to make me realize how important steps really are.

Soon I was working at a boot camp. What a change that was, for there was no physical labor involved. While there my coaching abilities were revived. You see, this program housed children (both male and female) ages seventeen to thirty-five. This was like getting a new group of kids playing softball. Most days I love my job, some days I do not, but I know with all my heart that God set my feet on Dixon Springs ground for a purpose, and that was to help the children. As I look back on my life, I can remember many role models along the way that have shaped me and molded me into the man I am today. One never knows what an effect we can have on another person's life by merely being a mentor. I have been blessed to the point of tears. The following are a series of short stories of my life and others who have helped me make this journey and have added spice in my life that makes my life complete. God has truly blessed me in this trip I call life. He gave wonderful parents and grandparents, as well as a good wife and children and grandchildren and three wonderful men in the lives of my daughters. It does not get better than that. Please join me as we make this trip.

Morris Document 2

As far back as I can remember, I haven't wanted much in this world. I did not ask for much as a kid, mainly because there was not much to be had. Raising four sons was a big job for my parents. We had some pretty lean times. Growing up in rural Southern Illinois, we didn't have all the things kids that lived in town had, so you made your own entertainment. Looking back on these times, it has come very clear to me that all that was really important to me was to be happy. I don't refer to money or material things; those things will never make you happy. I mean being happy and having that smile on your face all the time. This lesson was taught to me by my mother and father as they raised me. They instilled in me some important lessons that I try to live by even today. A lesson they taught me was if someone didn't have a smile, simply give them one, to share my happiness with others. Or if someone had a hard heart for whatever reason, try to soften it with kindness. I have always enjoyed smiling, but I also enjoyed making others smile. I guess this is why God gave me a sense of humor, so I could make a person laugh. I don't want to sound boastful, but I would go to great lengths to get a laugh out of someone that was having a bad day or was just sour on the world.

    This way of thinking carried me through school to leave the farm and finally into the US Navy. After completing my schools, I was assigned to the USS *Brumby* stationed at Charleston, South Carolina. When I arrived in Charleston, the ship was not there; it was in Cuba. I remember being so homesick I threw up many times, for I had never been away from home before. Finally, I was flown to Cuba to join my ship. It was rough the first three days. No one spoke to me much, and I felt very alone. Just as I felt I was losing my mind, came this man that seemed to have noticed how lonely I was. He stuck that huge hand out to me and said, "They call me Hot-Dogger." My fears began to melt, and I felt like one of the guys. Our friendship would last the entire time we were in the navy together. You see, he had shared a smile with me when I needed one badly. I think of all the times this recipe has worked while in the navy. Mom and Dad had steered me in the right direction as they have many times in my life. No matter where in this world, even to foreign countries, this philosophy works. No matter what place of employment I had—the navy, working twenty years in a coal mine, working at the VA hospital, or working at my present job at a boot camp—these simple lessons have spoken to me and carried me always. My ability to see humor in most any situation has pulled me up when I was down and possibly helped others. We never know what a difference our positive words, thoughts, and actions have on another person. We may all have a Hot-Dogger in our lives and don't even know it. I can never be able to thank my parents enough for all the things they have done for me over the years. I thank God I was fortunate enough to be their son. I have so many stories in my life that I feel should be told, not to make me look good, but to make someone that hasn't smiled in a while smile, or to make someone find the moral of the story and see the world in a new light. I am a firm believer that all things happen for a reason, that people are put in our paths for a reason; this is God's master plan. We never know if a person is an angel that was put into our path for a reason. This is the reason I try to treat people as best as I can. The stories you are about to read are true stories. I know they are true because I lived them. Some are funny, while some happened to me to teach what God was trying to tell me. Some of the stories really had no meaning to me at that time, only another page in my past only to dawn on me one day maybe some years later. This has happened to me many times when a preacher preaches his Sunday message, and I would wonder what he was trying to tell me, then one day it would click and I would suddenly realize what he was trying to say. Many of these stories are this way.

Morris Document 3

Let Your Stories Live Through Yourself

From the time I was born, I have had the good fortune of having rubbed elbows with some of the most wonderful people and also some that were not so wonderful. God has allowed me to remember these stories to the minutest detail, and I could remember most of the details and circumstances of which they occurred. Over the past years, he began to tell me I should write these stories down for someday I would come to the point in my life when I would forget them and they would be lost for my children and grandchildren to somehow get to know the man I was. God has blessed me with many opportunities in my life here on earth and has allowed me so many good memories along the way. These blessings are the spice in my life that cheers me when I'm sad and makes me laugh when I don't feel like laughing.

Another reason I can remember these things is the fact that I am bipolar. A person afflicted with this brain disease has the ability to be creative to the point it sometimes scares me. This disease to me is a blessing, for there is no way I feel I can accomplish the things I do if not for this disorder. God sometimes puts things like this in our lives to shape and mold us into what he has in store for our lives. Sometimes we ignore these talents, and they are lost. Many times the stories of our lives are a direct reflection of who we are if we choose to view ourselves this way, and if God is not in our lives, these reflections become clouded. On our walk through this life, we are faced with many decisions. Of these decisions, I feel the most important one is to follow Jesus Christ, for he is the cornerstone to a successful and happy life. If it weren't for Christ, I feel I would wander aimlessly in this world with no direction and would have missed all the opportunities I have been blessed with. Please join me as you read this book, for this is my life as I see it. Many stories will make you laugh, while a few may make you cry. I encourage you to write your own stories so you can pass this valuable information on to those that love you, and they can somehow understand why you are the way you are. This is especially true for the bipolar person and can possibly help encourage those afflicted with the disease and also help those who struggle to understand them.

Morris Document 4

My Time

Everyone has their own special quiet times where they can go and meditate, where they can be by themselves and deal with whatever problems life has to offer. I am no different. My quiet time is in the darkness of the early morning. This is the time I need to be away from everyone and the pressures of life. It is during these times of solitude I think of my wife, three daughters, and grandchildren, Mom and Dad, and my three brothers. It is also the time I feel my closest to God. This is when I do my deep thinking about life and the many mysteries it has to offer. This pattern began as a young man on the farm. During these times, I would always be up, ready to face the new day with an eagerness and need to see the warmth of that sun as it split the eastern sky. This carried on through my school years and continued with me as I entered the US Navy. After my schools were complete, I finally was assigned to a ship and found myself at sea. While at sea, I found myself wanting to rise in the darkness, go on the main deck, and be perched on the bow of this big ship to witness the sunrise.

You see, I view the sunrise different than most. I see the face of God as it would come up out of that calm ocean. For you see, as the glow of the presun came, I felt assured it was going to rise and give me that peace of the resurrection. Sometimes the sea was stormy, as our lives sometimes get stormy, but the face of God is always there, but sometimes we are so wrapped up in this world and its problems that we cannot or will not notice. I view the sunrise and the setting of the sun different, I guess, for you see, I see the setting of the sun as the death of Christ and its rising as his promise to return. As the sun rises each day, I feel the warmth and comfort of his presence that only God can give. This is the reason I want the experience of the rising sun in my daily life as much as possible. Few have the opportunity to experience the sun coming out of the ocean or the setting of it into a dark sea, but as far as the experience I have gained from these events, they are ones I wouldn't trade for all the riches this world has to offer. I am not saying everyone should rise up early each day to see the sun come up, for everyone is not like me, but if you need an eye-opening experience that comes with a sunrise, just try it, for it may change your view as far as this hectic world we live in.

Morris Document 6

He Wasn't Always My Hero

When I was young, I had the usual heroes young boys my age had: Superman, the Lone Ranger, the good guys we called them. I was in need of a role model, someone who was always there for me. My dad worked so much that he couldn't be there for me at those ballgames or the school plays, the events I felt were much more important than a field full of hay or a new calf. The years went by, and I began to feel left out. I wasn't depressed as I remember. I needed to be noticed a little more than an occasional butt busting he gave me. I can remember thinking at times he was the meanest man to draw air, but I knew that wasn't true. Soon I was in high school, and the time began to fly. He began to give me more and more responsibilities. This mean man I knew began to transform into a teacher, then a dad. Shortly before I graduated, I signed up to enlist in the US Navy. This would change many things for me.

As the days passed, I began to wonder when my dad would pull me to the side and give me this big speech as far as where to go and not to go. For you see, he too was a veteran of the navy. Finally, August 26, 1971 came. Mom and Dad drove me to the bus station. My dad shook my hand and gave me a hug. I still had no speech or words of wisdom to take with me on this journey. As he put me on this bus, he said three words to me. He looked me straight in the eye and said, "Watch your company." I got on that bus, feeling as if I had been cheated. I felt I had no tools to take with me on this trip that took me away from home for the first time in my life. Those three words soon began to shape me and mold me into a young man that soon began to realize what a valuable piece of advice my dad had given me. For you see, those three words carried me to many places around this world. When the guys wanted to drink a beer, go to a whorehouse, or smoke a joint, I would hear this speech in the back of my head. "Watch your company" would echo in the back of my mind. It never failed me then, and it still remains there today. That three-word speech has become ingrained in my very soul. As I grow older, I can only hope and pray that I can one day have the wisdom and knowledge that I see in my dad. He truly is a great man that corrected when he had to and gave advice and wisdom when he needed to. My dad is eighty-two years old. I still go to him for advice. I need his approval even today. This man is my best friend.

Morris Document 7

Tear Up the Ticket

July 14, 2002, started out like any other day for me. As usual, I was running late to go to work, trying to shower, eat, and get my uniform on and run out the back door. My path this day would take me south to Creal Springs to New Burnsides, on to Vienna, and finally to the boot camp where I worked. As usual I had the AC in full blast, the radio loud, running ninety miles per hour, with my hair on fire. About halfway to Creal, this still small voice came to me and said, "I want you to speak at your dad's funeral." So I did what any other lukewarm Christian and halfway decent son would do. I finally realized it was the Lord talking to me, so instead of running from him, I reached up and turned the radio off and tried to listen to him. He began to tell me some things about my dad, some I already knew, while some things I didn't know or had simply forgotten. In the days to come, I would smother my dad, for in my mind, his time would be soon at hand. I had even told some of my family that we would soon lose Dad. Our schedule and God's schedule are very different. He doesn't tell us, or we can't predict our time to leave. The only thing we can be sure of is to be ready when the time comes. I was down at Dad's every chance I got, for this time could be the last time. I remember one day in particular, we had no dew. I was mowing by 8:00 a.m. When I looked toward the field where Dad kept his cattle, his truck was still there; it was 9:30. Anyone who knows my dad knows that he goes to the bottom, as he calls it, at 8:00 a.m., and he stays thirty minutes and then he goes back home to check on Mom.

As I saw how late it was, so I shut the mower off and went to my truck and began that mere quarter-mile ride to the field. As I drove, my eyes began to search the field for my dad. I asked myself, "Is this the morning the Lord has been preparing me for?" Finally I pulled up behind my dad's truck. The mirror was full of my dad's face. He was slumped over against the door, and his eyes were shut. I couldn't move. Finally, I got up enough courage to get out of my truck and began to ease up the side of my dad's truck. I had put up my right hand and was going to check my dad's pulse and see if he was warm or cold. Just as I reached his neck, those blue eyes came open, and he said, "What are you doing, boy?"

After I came down, I didn't know whether to hug him or hit him. What had happened that bright, sunny morning as the truck faced the east was that he simply fell asleep. He got out of the truck, and we went to the gate and stood there and talked about those cattle that grazed so peacefully on that beautiful pasture, and I asked him why he came down here every day. "The cattle are on grass and they have plenty of water, so why come every day?"

He then looked at me and said, "You don't get it, do you?"

I asked, "Get what?"

He went on to say, "This is where I come not only to think about my cattle but also to think about my family, my wife, my four sons and their families, and my mom and dad and brothers and sisters, who have gone on before me." You see, my dad didn't go to church with Mom much, but as we stood there with our feet on that gate, it came so clear to me as I looked out across that field that this was my dad's church. And suddenly my fears about my dad's salvation began to fade. I still have my dad. He is eighty-four. His health is failing. He can't hear or see very well, but he is still, other than my wife, my best friend. I never told Dad about what I thought that warm summer morning, but I bet he would have laughed. So I have no problem speaking at my dad's funeral. There are some things I want to share about my dad that some people may not know. He has been a wonderful father and friend to me. He has been the one I go to for help, not just a loan when I needed it, but he loaned me advice many times when I knew not what to do. Or when I was scared, he was there to calm my fears. When I would ask him what I owed him, he would simply say, "Tear up the ticket."

Over the years I have watched him teach us boys some important lessons in life. Some of these came attached to a belt, which was no doubt deserved. These lessons didn't hurt me; they, on the other hand, helped me understand my faults and see things Dad's way. Thank you for caring enough to correct me. So as I think about Dad, I must say how much I love him, and when his time comes, I'll miss him, but now I know that someday I'll see him again.

Morris Document 8

He Went by GB

Once there was a man who had a tremendous influence on my life as a boy and would carry on into my adult life. This man worked all his life on a 320-acre farm, as well as worked construction during the day. He did all this work without ever complaining once for he loved the farm with a deep passion. When times were rough, he bought five hundred chickens so he could sell the eggs to the area restaurants. What a job it must have been to wash all those eggs. He also would sell sausages to whomever needed it; he had hogs also. He was a generous man as well, for I have been told many times that he would give food to someone who was hungry, and he did this without being paid or complaining. He did not smoke or drink like many men would do; he simply worked. He seemed his happiest when he was working on his farm for this farm had been his lifelong dream. I would hear stories of how he would help a neighbor who was sick and could not care for his crops or livestock. GB would be right there to help however he could. He was never paid for any of this, nor would he ask for pay.

He was a good husband to his wife. Together they raised four sons on this farm, and they would go on to be married over sixty years. He was a strict father to those four boys and would be quick to correct them but also quick to forgive and tell them why they had gotten in trouble. I never heard of this man getting into any fights. This man had only an eighth-grade education, but he held a master's degree in people. He was a very good judge of character; he could read you like a book. As I watched him work cattle, I noticed how easy he was with those cows. I then thought this must be the same gentleness he demonstrated with his children. Those cattle would go to become his children after the boys married and left the farm. He would groom them, and I have seen him talk to them. If the truth was known, I would say he had names for all of them. As the years went by and age began to stack up on him, he knew the day was coming that he would have to part with his cattle. His eyesight was failing, as well as his hearing was leaving, plus he had to help care for his wife, who was in poor health. Finally, the day came when they would come to haul his cattle away. I saw tears running down his face as they loaded his babies up. The real tears flowed when the last load rolled off the arm. A chapter of his life had closed, one that had been opened sixty-four years earlier. I once asked him why he felt he had to go to the field every morning. "The cows have grass and plenty of water, so why come here each day?"

He looked at me and said, "You don't get it, do you?"

I said, "Get what?"

He then shocked me when he said, "This is the time I not only check on the cows but I also go by my sons' houses and think about my wife and all of our family and think of my mom and dad and my brothers and sisters who have gone on before me."

Suddenly, as I stood there with my foot propped up on that gate, I realized that this place was his church, where he brought his burdens and spent time with God. At that moment, I was at peace about my friend's salvation. This friend I speak of with so much respect is my father—the guy who has always been there for me and given me advice and guidance and also correction when I needed them, which was often. Someday when the time comes, I feel led to speak at my dad's funeral, for I feel there are some things that need to be said about this great man who never once complained over the fifty-three years he has been in my life. My dad and I have a great relationship as well, both being navy veterans. Sometimes we discuss times past at sea. I can talk to my dad about anything and still value his wisdom even today. I only hope that one day I can be half the man that my dad is and hope he passes some of his wisdom to me so I can pass it on to my children and grandchildren. My dad has left me with a fortune, not dollars, but a vast supply of knowledge, wisdom, and patience, so he made me rich. When the time comes for my dad to leave this world, I will be lost, but I feel a part of my dad lives in me, so I will always have him with me no matter where my steps lead me. Someday I will cross paths with this great man in a much greener pasture where his eyesight and hearing will be perfect.

Morris Document 9

He Gave Me a Present on His Birthday

December 17, 2003

Today is the eighty-second birthday of my dad, G. B. Morris. I went down there early this morning, as I do many mornings. This particular day, I had some business I needed to discuss with him. You see, last Friday, Dennis had taken Dad to Vienna, Illinois, to take his driver's test. I later learned Dad had failed his test; he had missed seven questions and ten road signs. You are allowed to test three times in the state of Illinois. Dad seemed irritated about this, saying he couldn't understand the questions and had been somewhat confused. He later told me on Sunday, the fourteenth, that he didn't need their license to drive. I thought, "Oh boy, here we go." So I dreaded talking with Dad about this issue.

The day of his birthday came. I went in and said hello to Mom, and she told me it was Dad's birthday. I could hear Dad in the basement, so I went downstairs to talk to him. As we began to talk, he seemed so calm and deliberate in his words. I mentioned to him that I would help him study and then take him to Vienna to retake his driving test. It was then that he shocked me, for he replied to me, "I don't want to hurt anyone. You boys can take me anywhere I need to go." He went on to tell me that he didn't need that old car anymore but that he would like to keep his old truck to check his cattle. He went on to say his memory was leaving, that he could read one page of the driver's book and go to the next page and not remember the previous page. I then asked Dad if he understood what he was telling me. He said he understood fully what he was saying. He said that sometimes these things had to happen as we got older.

I am so proud of my dad for being wise enough to see these things and so fortunate for being able to be part of his life. So you see, on my dad's eighty-second birthday, I'm the one who received the gift!

Morris Document 10

Steps

Have you ever thought about steps? I mean, the ones we use every day in our daily lives? Steps are the vehicles that take us up and down. They take us higher and lower to get us where we need to go. They seem so insignificant to us; we simply take them for granted. I had never really sat down and thought much about steps.

My story really began in the spring of 2005. Our youngest daughter had announced she was getting her own apartment. She was a young college student setting out on her own. I had told her I would help her move, as I had with her two sisters before her. Our nest would be empty for the first time since 1977. She had chosen to move to Carbondale and room with her lifelong girlfriend. I remember that day as I drove to her apartment, my mind wandered back over the many memories of my three daughters, all the good times, the laughter, and sometimes the tears that go along with raising these wonderful ladies. I wondered how we kept our sanity sometimes, but we had. Suddenly, I see the brake lights of my daughter's car. We had arrived at her new home. As I got out of my truck, I realized what section of town we were in. I tried not to act worried. Then as she opened the door to lead me to her apartment, my real surprise came. I saw before me the longest, steepest set of steps I have ever seen in my life! As I carried dressers, boxes, and all the stuff a young college girl has to have to live with, I counted those steps. There were twenty-one. By the end of this move, I was exhausted, but I said nothing except to be careful going up and down the steps. A year and some months later, I would climb those steps to mover her back home. I have never been so happy to move someone in my life. I never once complained.

This story never had much of an effect on me at that time. It was just another page in my past. But recently it took on a new meaning for me. I began to look at steps in a totally different way. You see, my life has been somewhat in a turmoil this past year. We had a house fire, we almost lost this same daughter to a car crash, and we had an attempted break-in. We stayed in a motel for thirty-nine days. I was off six weeks from work with a burned hand. Add all these things up with all the other stresses of everyday life and you have a perfect recipe for overload. I ended up in the hospital with exhaustion and stress. While in the hospital, I had the chance to focus on my life. I began to see things in a different light.

One night as I lay in my bed, I thought of that long, steep set of steps to my daughter's apartment. As I closed my eyes, I could picture them, how steep they were and how many of them there were. I thought of my life this past year. How many steps has is taken me to get to where I am now? How many times had I been knocked down the steps? Suddenly it occurred to me what steps really are. I used to view steps as vehicles that take us up or down to take us where we need to go. I know now this was wrong. I was seeing it all wrong. God put that long, steep, dangerous set of steps in my path not to make me rise above anyone or take me to a higher station in life; he simply put these steps in my path to slow me down, to make me see life in a new light. He was telling me to slow down and enjoy the ride. Now I see my life in a totally different light. I can look back on the right path. These are the times I grew, the times he showed me the many things I have to be thankful for, and all the wonderful people I have had the opportunity to rub elbows with along the way. I know now things don't just happen by accident. All things happen for a reason. I know for sure now why my wonderful daughter chose that rundown apartment in Carbondale—so this old man could get a clear view of those wonderful steps that were before me!

Morris Document 11

Her Name Was Mary

I once knew this woman who had a great influence on my life that she might never know. She was a simple woman who never drew attention to herself in any way. She merely wanted to make a difference in the lives she came in contact with. This lady based her life on Jesus Christ, and he radiated in her daily life. She would put others before herself at all times and never complained the first time. She never smoked or drank or even wore makeup or drove a car; she wanted that simple life of a housewife, mother, and grandmother. She would have four sons, so you could see she was outnumbered in her home. She was always asked if she felt cheated because she had no daughters. She would respond that the Lord must have seen she needed all these boys, so she'd deal with what he had sent her. She was a perfect role model for all mothers to follow, for one could see what an influence she had on many lives that came in contact with her. She was a strict mother to those four boys and was quick to correct them when they needed it but also was quick to forgive and go on with life. She wouldn't even allow those boys to call their father the old man; that was not allowed. She would cook and clean without the help of anyone, and she would do all the laundry that was generated by a husband and four sons, again without any complaining. She could sing like a bird as she did her work in the house. She had written many songs herself, and she would sing to the Lord for she sought not an audience. She never wanted much in this world as far as wealth or possessions for her wealth was in her family and relationship with God. So she was one of the wealthiest women I knew. The ones around her were the lucky ones to have the opportunity of rubbing elbows with her, for she could calm even the stormiest storms with the words spoken so softly. She would be married for over sixty years to the same man, the only man she ever loved. She once said she wouldn't change her life for anything in this world, and I was sure she meant this with all her heart. This lady would never gossip about those around her or say even a cross to anyone. I am sure there were times when living on that farm that she felt lonely and depressed, but her faith in God sustained her, and she went on with his work she felt led to do. She set a good example for all to see, for it was magnified in her life. She had the perfect example to follow for her parents lived the same type of life she led. They are proud, I'm sure, as they look down and see her lead her life on this earth, for she has run a good race. I am sure that one day when her time comes, she will see them again. She will have a new body and mind and have a great time. This person still speaks to me even though she doesn't talk much anymore, but I am sure she hears everything that goes on around her. I am so blessed to say this person is my mother. She has given me much more than I can ever pay back to her, but knowing her, I'm sure she would tell me the debt has already been paid. That is just the way she is. Her name is Mary!

Morris Document 12

Our Towrope

It's May 1973; the ship I am on is on a towrope in the North Atlantic. I'm a twenty-year-old second-class hull tech aboard the USS *Brumby* in the US Navy. The story you are about to hear is a true story. No one has heard this story before; it has been locked away for over twenty-five years in my mind. The real meaning has never become apparent to me until lately.

The real story began in 1971; I was a mere kid of eighteen, fresh out of high school. I had decided to enlist in the navy, partly to escape my seemingly boring life on the farm I grew up on in deep Southern Illinois and partly to follow in the footsteps of my father, who had also enlisted in the navy. My motive was as I had mentioned; his was World War II.

After enlisting in the navy, I attended firefighting school; I then went to welding school. After my schools were completed, I was assigned to the USS *Brumby* (DE-1044), home-ported in Charleston, South Carolina. My first two years went fairly fast. I advanced rapidly, and soon I was in charge of a small repair with eight men to oversee. The Vietnam war was going full blast, but all the naval action was from the West Coast. The East Coast seemed immune at this time.

By this time, it is January 1973. We had just received our orders to ship out for a ninety-day NATO cruise. This cruise would take us deep into the North Atlantic. The three-month trip would break the boredom of being in port; we looked forward to some new surroundings. Our assignment was to operate with some British ships and conduct at-sea drills and tests for our systems and training. About midway into the cruise, our twin smokestacks began to blow white smoke. Some tubes in our propulsion system had salted up, and our boilers had failed. There we were, dead in the water, adrift in the choppy North Atlantic. We were soon towed up the Firth of Clyde and anchored in the harbor at Faslane, Scotland. For the next three months, we were in limbo, waiting to see what they would do with us. Scotland is a very pretty country. The people are warm and friendly, and they made us feel welcome. Our two choices were to either go to South Hampton shipyards in England or be towed across the Atlantic to a dry dock in Charleston, South Carolina. Finally, the word came down; we were to be towed home. Soon, more word came that the married men would be sent home via another ship, and the single men and essential personnel would remain onboard the *Brumby*. I was a single man at that time; also, I was in charge of firefighting and damage control training on board. I was not surprised to be among the half of the crew that was ordered to remain on board.

At last an oceangoing tug arrived from Dam Neck, Virginia. They estimated it would take us thirty-five to forty-five days to make the 38,000-plus-mile trip. The tug was capable of pulling us from three to five knots, somewhat slower than the twenty-nine knots we normally sailed at. After almost a week at sea, a weather forecast came to us, warning of a typhoon forming at sea. We were assured we would be well clear of its path. By 4:00 p.m. that afternoon, it was very apparent they had been very wrong. That particular day, I was assigned the midwatch. I was to assume the watch at midnight and continue until 4:00 a.m. At 5:00 p.m., the seas had become very rough. They had ordered all watertight hatches secured, and no one was to be on the main deck. At 7:00 p.m., I decided to go get some sleep before my watch. My rack was on the bottom, with two racks above me, and by 8:00 p.m., I had been thrown out of my rack three times. I finally gave up and went to the bridge where they steer the ship. We were now in thirty-foot seas, and we were taking thirty-five- to forty-degree rolls. You could not keep your trays on the tables in the mess decks or walk down the passageways.

SUNRISE

At midnight, I assumed my watch. Sound and security watch consists of carrying a .45-caliber automatic pistol, two full clips, and a sounding tape. The sounding tape is used to check the voids in the bottom of the ship; these voids keep the ship floating. Any detection of water would tell you that damage has caused a leak. My first two hours were uneventful; the sea was getting rougher. At 2:00 a.m., I went to report into the bridge to tell them all was secure. As I entered the bridge, Seaman Otis Moore, a huge black man, was at the helm, steering the ship. As I moved behind him, he said, "Tow broke." At first it didn't register what he meant, but as I looked straight off the bow, I realized I didn't see the familiar bright light on the stern of the tug. I can't describe the horror I felt when I realized the towline was severed. We were drifting in thirty-foot seas, without power in the middle of a typhoon. I remember thinking of home, my girlfriend, and my parents. Would I ever see them again? As fear began to flood into me, I gazed off to my far left. There was a bright glowing light that seemed to reach out to me. It was the stern of the tug, and suddenly fear was replaced with hope. None of us slept the rest of the night, but as sunrise approached, the seas began to subside. A bright sun emerged from a wonderfully calm ocean. What a beautiful sight for a bunch of scared, homesick sailors. We were attached to the tug and continued our journey home.

This account I endured really had no impact on me at that time. It was only another page in my past. Now I am forty-eight years old. I have a wonderful wife, a nice home, and three wonderful daughters. Recently, one of my daughters went through some stormy times in college. I went to her in hopes I could talk to her and tell her that life is very similar to the weather. Sometimes it storms till we think there is no hope things will ever get better. But the storms of life, like the typhoons of the sea, have to run their course. Storms are usually short-lived. The sun will eventually come out. We only have to remind ourselves of that.

As the years have gone by, I have realized another lesson I was taught that stormy night in the North Atlantic: when the storms come in my life, as long as my towrope is attached, I can weather any storm. The towrope I'm referring to is God. That night, my ship was adrift, but as I saw that light off to the left, comfort came over me. That night the tug was where it was supposed to be; it was our ship that was off course. How many times in my life have I drifted off course? God was not the one who severed the towline; it has always been me who lost the grip. God, like the tug, is there for us. We simply have to seek him out. Even if we have God, the storms are going to come, but if we can always keep our towline attached, we can weather any storm. Sometimes our storms of life help us to realize what is really important in life and cause us to really look at ourselves and count our blessings.

Morris Document 13

His Name Was Kenny

It was 3:00 a.m. My ship was tied to the pier in Kharg Island, Iran. After a long day at sea, we had made it to this small refueling depot in the Red Sea. I was alone in the shop I ran. I was enjoying the quietness as the hectic day finally came to an end. My mind was on my girlfriend and home, when I heard someone at the door. As the door swung open, I saw a man with a .45-caliber pistol. He was a young man that worked for me in this small shop. As I looked him in the eyes that early morning, he said, "I'm going to kill them." You see, two electronics techs that were drunk had slapped him around as they had boarded the ship a few minutes earlier. He had loaded the weapon and gone below decks. I'm not sure why he had chosen to come to the ship. I started to get up and try to get to the door. This was when he pointed the gun at me, and I sat back down. As our eyes met in a stare that seemed like it lasted forever, I asked him if that was the same gun I had on my watch the previous night, because it if was, it had jammed on me. To my surprise, he handed me the gun. I cleared the weapon and even talked him into giving me the other clip. I told him to sit down and gave him some coffee, and I ran as fast as I could to my division officer's quarters. I told him what was going on, and he immediately ordered men to go to the shop and take him into custody.

That next morning, he was airlifted from our ship and written up on a section 8. I've often wondered about that night. Why did he not simply go to their berthing space and shoot them? Why had he gone the wrong way and come to the shop? As I think back on this night, I know why our paths crossed that dark night in Iran. It was meant to be. You see, God sees all and knows all. Our meeting was not just a coincidence; it was all planned. You see, many lessons like this one have not been revealed to me until I was receptive enough to understand them. Sometimes our vision is so clouded with the pressures of life that we are blind. I often stop to think how this night could have turned out really bad, then I realize I had nothing to fear because someone far greater than me was in charge.

Morris Document 14

In Sight of the Shore

It was the summer of 1994. My family had decided to go on vacation in Destin, Florida. So we loaded up our van, complete with luggage, my wife and three daughters, and the oldest daughter's then boyfriend and a girlfriend of our middle daughter. I wonder now how we hauled all that stuff. Me, being the hardhead I am, decided I would drive straight through so we could get their quickly and start having fun. By the time we got there, I was so tired and crabby no one wanted to be around me. We had rented a condo that was near the beach; we bought food and soda and settled in for a well-deserved vacation. We went to the beach daily and were comfortable there on the beach near the shore.

One day we decided to rent some Jet Skis and venture out away from the shore for a different type of fun. We rented two skis; our middle daughter was upset because we were told you had to be sixteen to operate a Jet Ski. So I had to take turns with trips, hauling my wife, the two fifteen-year-olds, and our youngest daughter, who was nine. After a few trips, I decided my oldest daughter and her then boyfriend would mount one of the skis, and I and our two remaining daughters would take the other and go outside the harbor and ride along the beach. To get to the beachfront, you must leave the safety of the harbor and pass through a narrow channel to get to the open water. It was great out there in the open water. We would race and jump waves and wave at the people on the beach and on the boats. We were having the time of our lives.

Suddenly, out of nowhere, a squall blew up. Lighting was all around us; the rain beat our bathing-suited bodies. The winds were at gale force; the sea turned rough. I immediately motioned to head to that safe harbor. By the time we reached the narrow channel, we saw we were not the only ones with that idea. There were all kinds of small craft seeking the same safe harbor; they were coming in on all sides. The sand was blowing as though we were in a sandblaster. I finally decided we would beach the Jet Skis and run for the sand dunes to protect ourselves. Our youngest daughter saw a motel several hundred yards up the sand and immediately started to run. She was terrified. I finally caught her and covered her with my body. After what seemed like hours but was only a few minutes, the storm passed. We all were accounted for and back in our condo and back to the safety of the shore. What had been so terrifying, we now could laugh about. We had simply experienced a small storm.

It's now seven years later; this seemingly insignificant story, now that I am older, has taken on a new meaning to me. I have learned to try always to stay near the shore, not to venture too far out of the harbor and to pay attention to the storms that pop up without warning. You see, God is my shore; he is my safe harbor. There is nothing wrong with venturing outside the harbor, but we need to keep sight of the shore. We chose that day to take an innocent trip, but we lost sight of the shore. How many times in our lives have we decided to turn our backs on the shore and sail out of the harbor? The good thing about God is, the shore is always there and the harbor never closes.

Morris Document 15

Just an Old Table

One day in 1979, my wife, Rene, came home and told me about an old table and chairs she had found east of Herrin, Illinois. She told me it would take quite a bit of work, but she felt it would look pretty in our dining room. We went and looked at it and bought it for $350. For the next three months, I worked on the table and chairs to refinish them. The chairs had red antiquing on them, but they had not done this to the table yet. The set was soon completed, and we moved it from the cold garage into the warmth of our home.

But there is much more to this story than what I have shared with you. You see, this old table has become the centerpiece of our family. It has been the place where my wife and I have made many decisions, where we have agreed and disagreed many times. When I sit at this table, I recall many heart-to-heart talks over the years with three daughters—important things like boyfriends, curfews, and what kind of car we really need to shop for.

But my best thoughts and memories are the meals served around this old table. The laughter we have shared and sometimes the tears this old table has absorbed on the surface are my most precious memories. Like this past Thanksgiving, we had all three daughters, complete with husband and two boyfriends, and both my parents and Rene's parents here. But the crowning moment was when my mother gave the Thanksgiving prayer. But we can't forget all the slumber parties complete with ten to fifteen girls. Or the helium balloons this old table has held for all the birthday parties over the years. And I wonder, what has held this old table together? I feel the glue that has held this old table together has been our family. Sometimes the glue was stretched thin, and there might have times when the glue wanted to run, but it stuck and stayed put. So as you can see, as I view this old table, I see much more than wood. I see each of you.

Morris Document 16

That First Kiss

Chris Blumenstock and Amanda

The year 1990 was a turning point for me as far as being a dad. Rene by this time had given me three wonderful daughters. Our lives had been transformed from pleasingly simple to wonderfully complicated. The day you are about to read about changed me forever.

Our oldest daughter Amanda was in the seventh grade. She was always an excellent student, always near the top of her class. She, along with her two sisters, made their mother and me very proud. This particular span of time, Amanda had this perm. I called it her poodle look. As you may have guessed, Dad didn't care that much for it, but this was the fad at that time. One day Amanda asked to go over to her boyfriend's house. His name was Chris Blumenstock. I was to pick her up at 4:00 p.m. They wanted to watch some movies. At 4:00 p.m. sharp, I pulled in the driveway in my old truck, the truck my children called the Old Rusty or the Old Brown Turd. As Amanda got in the passenger's side, I heard a smack. She then closed the door, and we backed out. As we drove home, I asked her if Chris had kissed her. She said, "He gave me a peck on the cheek." This was when the dad talks started. I tried to explain to my oldest daughter that up until this point in her life, there had been no other men and how hard it was for a dad to see his daughter grow up. As we drove and talked, we both shed some tears, but neither took our eyes off the road.

As the years have passed, I have realized that afternoon was an episode in the rite of passage. It was only a little girl trying to become a young woman and a dad that was refusing to turn loose of that same little girl.

As we neared our home, I reached out and held my daughter's hand. As I held it, I softly but firmly told her, "We need to clean our faces up so Mom won't see us like this!" We both had a good laugh that day.

Morris Document 17

She's My Boy

On June 24, 1979, my wife gave birth to a daughter; she was our second daughter. She had big eyes and small features, but there was something different about this little girl. As she joined our family, I began to notice even at a very young age how independent she was. Most babies want to be rocked and sung to; this one wanted her huggy and wanted to be put in her piggie. For those of you who require translation, that's "Give me my diaper to suck my thumb with and put me in my bed." As the years went by, she soon turned into her own person. As the school years came, she was the one who had that magnetic personality that her classmates were attracted to. I remember one summer she and I were down at my dad's. My dad had bought some candy while he was in town and gave it to my daughter. That day she had only a small halter top and some tiny shorts. Several minutes passed, my dad asked for some of the candy he'd brought her. Looking confused, she reached insider her shorts and pulled out the candy. The surprised look on my dad's face was priceless. Our daughter said simply, "Papa, I didn't have any pockets!" I believe that was the last time my dad asked her for candy!

When she was five, she came to me one day, wanting to go squirrel hunting. I said I would take her; we loaded up in the truck and drove to the woods. As I started into the woods that day, she was fumbling around at the mouth of the woods. I called to her. Finally she emerged with a long stick. This was her rifle, and she wanted to be like me. I told her we would take one squirrel only that day. I located the squirrel and showed it to her and shot it. She ran over to it and started to pick it up. I stopped her and showed her how to make certain it was dead. She then shocked me when she wanted to carry it. I again told her to carry it by the tail, and we proceeded to the truck. She then asked if she could ride in the back. I asked why. She told me she just wanted to. I agreed, and we started home.

In my rearview mirror, I watched in delight as she would hoist the day's kill as we passed every house. This was my boy! She grew and matured. On through school she went—all the cheerleading, softball, boys, good and bad experiences of growing up—and she remained this independent person. This girl is a clone of my wife, but she is also somewhat like me. When I look back over the years, this daughter has given me so much joy. Sure there have been rough times, but the good far outweigh the bad. She has been my arrowhead hunter, my hunting buddy, even my fishing buddy. My other daughters have to. I don't want them to feel left out, but they, as well as I, know this daughter has been my boy. Something I should add to substantiate my theory: she owns a pickup truck, a four-wheeler, and she owns a camper down on the river!

Morris Document 18

Paid in Full

In 1976, I bought an old knife from a sweet old lady I was renting a piece of property from in Marion, Illinois. This lady had handed me the knife one day and asked me if I knew anything about knives. As I looked at the knife that day, I knew something was different about it, for it had thin butt plates, green side plates, and a diamond embedded in the side. But the biggest surprise came when I opened the knife. On the big blade was engraved one word: *Winchester*. My eyes focused on that word. I knew this knife was valuable to the right person. I showed this old knife one day to my oldest brother. He showed some interest and offered me some small amount for it. I laughed and declined. Later on my brother called me one night and asked if I would interested in a job at the coal mine he worked at. I jumped at the chance. He instructed me on what to do. It was a welding job; I took my welding test and passed. It wasn't long till they called me for the job; I would stay at this job for the next twenty-plus years.

My brother and I had always been close. We enjoyed doing the same things—fishing, hunting, collecting things. On February 25, 1985, this would change. After work that day, I was about three minutes behind my brother. As I turned off the entrance road to the main highway, I saw his truck off the side of the road ahead. Another man flagged me over. As I pulled up in front of my brother's truck, I could see he was slumped over to the left side of his truck. I went around to the passenger's side and opened the door and got in. I began to tear at his clothes so he could get some air. At this point I told the other guy to get an ambulance. I kept telling him I could hear the ambulance coming. He was choking by this time; I thought he would choke to death in my lap. Soon an EMT from the mines arrived. She assessed him with a stroke on the right side. This stroke would affect him the rest of his life; suddenly he was changed into a person I wasn't sure I knew. He seldom joked or cut up like we used to do. I guess I was the one who had trouble adjusting.

The years rolled by, and suddenly it was twenty-eight years since that old knife was purchased. I had tried numerous times to locate this collector where I could make a bunch of money. Also, during these times, I have rubbed this knife in front of my brother's face with the same results. During this time, my dad had decided to quit driving, but not totally. He had failed his driving test but continued to drive some. I had gone to my dad's this day to tell him his insurance wasn't any good and he risked a lawsuit if he was involved in an accident. It was there that morning that another idea came to me. It had suddenly come to me that I knew this perfect collector I sought. It was my own brother; I went directly home and got the knife. For almost twenty-eight years, the knife had been kept in the finger of an old jersey glove I had cut off. I went to my brother's home that morning and made small talk about dad. I then told my brother I had something I wanted him to have. I handed him the old glove finger. He asked in his gruff voice, "What's that?" As he pulled the old knife from that fancy case, his eyes lit up. He then told me he'd give thirty-five dollars for the knife. I told him if he tried to give money for it, that I wanted it back. I then told him that he was the knife collector I had been hunting for all this time. He asked me why I would give him such a knife. I told him that many years ago, a man had gotten me a job in the coal mines, a job that had built my home and raised my children. It was just a small way of saying thank you. As I left to go out the door that day, he was trying to pay me for the knife. I turned and told him as I closed the door, "It's paid in full."

Morris Document 19

She Taught Me This Day

My wife and I are blessed with three beautiful daughters. I have pleasant memories of each of these girls. When I get one of these memories in mind, I try to jot it down. This morning I glanced at some pictures of our youngest daughter. Immediately a story came to mind. I was transported back to the year 1993. My wife had asked me to run to the grocery store for her and get some items for a Sunday dinner. Our youngest daughter quickly jumped to her feet to accompany me on this trip. As we drove, we talked about softball, school, and things of interest to her. We soon arrived at the grocery store and began to look for the things on the grocery list. Men have to carry a list even if the list has only one item; it's a guy thing, I guess. My wife doesn't know this, but many times I would write on the palm of my hand so I wouldn't look stupid. This particular Sunday morning, it was very crowded. It was warm outside, so I guess everyone was cooking out for dinner. Our path this morning took us down the side of a large salad bar. This particular salad bar was twenty-five feet long and seven feet wide. As we looked at the many items on this huge bar, I noticed a large container of black olives sitting there in the ice. The container looked as big as a five-gallon bucket. Black olives is a weakness for me. I could eat them all day long. As we went past the olives, I glanced behind me also to the left and right. At this point, I swiped one of the olives and crammed it in my mouth as we went down the aisle. It was at this point my world exploded. My eight-year-old daughter hit me with a sledge hammer. She said, "Dad, you're not setting a very good example for me." She was laughing as she said this. I stopped dead in my tracks and turned around and grabbed her by the shoulders. Tears began to well up in my eyes as I looked down into the eyes of my child. I told her she was right and that I was the one who was wrong. For you see, I was to be her role model, but this day, she had taught me. For you see, this day I had taught my daughter it was okay to steal. Whether it was that black olive or a car, stealing is stealing; the concept is the same. We as parents have to be so very careful what message we send in our daily walks with our children. They don't miss a word we say or an action we do. The abovementioned story is one of my favorite memories of my young daughter, for you see, this was the day the daughter corrected the dad.

Morris Document 20

The Old Ugly Pie Safe

In 1985, while on a mission to buy an old piano for my daughters, I stumbled across an old pie safe. This piece of furniture was without question the ugliest single piece I had ever considered refinishing. I ended up buying the pie safe, the piano, and an old one-seat school desk for the grand total of twenty-five dollars. After getting the pieces home, I left the old pie safe out in the garage to work on later. While out there, one day I looked at it; it had at least four coats of paint on it, some green, some pink. Even the six tin panels had been painted. I attempted to strip one door, but I became so depressed with the amount of work that was involved that I walked away in disgust. The old safe would sit in the garage for the next nine years, till one day I made up my mind to start on it. All the joints on the piece were loose. All the hardware was tarnished; even the inside had been painted I didn't know where to start.

    Piece by piece I began to work on the pie safe. I suddenly began to notice how old this piece really was. The paint and varnish were off, the hardware had the tarnish removed, all the joints were reglued, and suddenly I began to see something I had not seen before. Finally, I was down to the six tin panels. This was the tedious part. I had to clean these holes out with a toothpick. I worked on these panels forever, till finally they were clean. I had restored the patina finish to them, and finally I was ready to stain and varnish. This old ugly pie safe, as I had named it, turned out to be the prettiest piece I have ever restored. After I had finished the pie safe, I began to look at the pictures I had taken before I had started to work on it. I remembered how I had all but given up on the safe because it was so ugly, how I didn't think it would ever amount to anything, and how I would walk by it without even noticing it.

I soon began to think how people are viewed the way I viewed this old pie safe. Maybe our clothes aren't the right brand, or they may be torn or dirty. Maybe the expression on our face shows anger, or our face shows rejection. Maybe the person just needs a kind word. Sometimes a simple word of encouragement is all that it takes to turn a life around.

So you see, through this old ugly pie safe, I was taught a lesson, that sometimes when we take off the layers of what life has put on us, we find some hidden beauty beneath. When I think back of me being afraid to work on the pie safe, I find myself wondering how many people I have passed by that I would not take the time to talk to because they didn't seem worthy. Or they had a coat of paint on them, or they simply just didn't look right. Sometimes a simple thing like the old ugly pie safe can open our eyes to things around us.

Morris Document 21

Her Special Touch

December 18, 2003

The old pie was finally finished; my wife and I carried it into the house. The last two weeks had been spent transforming an old ugly pie safe that was painted with loose joints into one that was straight, tight, and stained. As we located it in our dining room, everyone spoke of how pretty it looked. In my mind I knew something was missing. It just didn't look right, but I said nothing. I left to go to work that day, still unsure of what it was that bothered me so much. All that day I thought about it, unable to put my mind to rest. Before I could turn around, it was time to come home. As I pulled up the drive that night, I could see my wife had been very busy. The Christmas lights were up outside, as well as the ribbons she always put up. I went inside into the kitchen; there I found her working on some more decorations. As she told me what all she had done that day, I glanced into our darkened dining room. It was then I saw something very beautiful. I raced into the dining room and turned on the light. There in front of me was that old pie safe. My wife had decorated it with her special touch, the touch only she has. This special touch has affected me for several years now.

When I was in grade school, there was this girl; she was different from any of the girls in school. She liked to fish and get muddy and was the best softball player of all the girls. Then in about the sixth grade, I started to like her for more than the qualities I mentioned. I noticed she was smart and pretty; she even lived real close to me. Later, on our eighth-grade trip to St. Louis, I would give her my identification bracelet. She accepted the bracelet; suddenly I had my first girlfriend. So we became an item, and all the way through high school we went. She would turn out to be the only I would ever date. Soon after high school was over, we parted ways for the first time. She moved to St. Louis, Missouri, to attend St. Luke's School of Nursing. I enlisted in the US Navy and was off to boot camp in Great lakes, Illinois. But she still affected me with her special touch.

Every time I could get to a phone, I would call her. The number in her dorm was 314-721-9544, and I will never forget that number. Soon I was out of boot camp and was transferred to Philadelphia, Pennsylvania. I came home in December 1971 for Christmas. On the east side of the Marion square in my dad's old '67 Chevy, I gave this same girl an engagement ring. She cried and accepted it and slipped it on her finger and wore it with her special touch. Soon I was transferred again to California, then on to Charleston, South Carolina. While in Charleston, I proposed over the phone to her, and she accepted. We went on to be married on April 28, 1973. After she graduated from nursing school, we finally got to live together. She worked to set up our first home, a tiny one-bedroom apartment. Her special touch made it a home. Before we could turn around, it was June 1975 and I was a free man. We threw everything into a moving van and headed for Illinois. My wife worked at Herrin Hospital. I went to college on the GI Bill. Soon I had my first real job as a welder working mine construction. Six months later, I would get a better job with Amax Coal. I would stay there for the next twenty years.

On March 2, 1977, something happened to us that changed our lives forever. At 3:55 a.m., our first daughter was born. She was the most beautiful thing I had ever held. My wife held her and nursed her, and again this special touch was exposed. Time passed, and we decided to move to the country and build a new home. Soon, another event took place that caused our world to rotate somewhat differently. On June 24, 1979, at 1:34 p.m., our second daughter was born; she too was perfect. She had big eyes; she still to this day looks just like her mother. So now my wife has to spread that special

SUNRISE

touch between two daughters and me. Just when the pressures of two daughters and husband that was far from perfect were taking its toll on her, along came October 8, 1985. At 9:50 p.m., our third daughter came roaring onto the scene. She wasn't like the other girls; she was simply herself. My wife's special touch has been very evident in the lives of our children.

Whether it was being a nurse to a sick child, organizing birthday parties, or those special productions at Halloween and Christmas, she's always been there. When I think back over the thirty-plus years of marriage, she's always wound my clock. Whether it's a meal, how she decorates, or in the many things she does for us all, or simply how she looks at me, she is special. Someday I'm sure she will again spread her special touch on her grandchildren. You see, this is the same girl that I knew in the eighth grade I would spend my life with!

Morris Document 22

The Perfect Gift

It's Christmastime 2003. Last-minute shopping is at full speed in our home. My wife is operating at breakneck speed because I haven't helped her much. Our oldest daughter had called about four days before Christmas and told my wife she had a big surprise for her. My phone rang in my pocket in the Walmart checkout lane; it was my wife. She had called to tell me of the conversation she had with our daughter, and she asked me what I thought. I simply said, "She's pregnant."

As we discussed this, we sort of joked with the idea of being grandparents. We even went to our workplaces and told everyone we were to be grandpa and grandma. Christmas Eve day finally comes with much anticipation. Our daughter calls me that morning as they drive home. She wants to know if everyone is at home and if they are out of bed. I tell her they are, and she talks a little longer, and we hang up. I race to my wife and tell her of our conversation. Finally they arrive, complete with their dog, and in come the presents. I anxiously await the blessed news. We then open their gifts to us and ours to them, still no baby news. Finally our daughter hands my wife a gift and says, "Here's your big surprise."

My wife says, "This is my surprise?" somewhat in shock. "We thought you was going to tell us you was going to have a baby."

"A baby?" our daughter says. "What made you think I was pregnant?"

What a big laugh we all had that morning.

Christmas comes and goes; it's now New Year's Day. We had taken our middle daughter to St. Louis to catch a plane to Texas. Our oldest daughter wanted us to come by for some ham and beans. We arrive at their home, and her husband greets us and says she is fixing her hair. We wait and wait. Finally she comes in and starts to get the table ready. I notice she is uneasy in her chair. Finally, she says, "I'm really pregnant this time."

My wife and I say, "Sure you are."

She tearfully says, "No, I mean I really am pregnant!"

By this time my wife is crying. My mouth is wide open; another twist in the big surprise saga has emerged. As it turned out, she really was pregnant Christmas Eve morning, but you see, we don't receive things on our timing. God has his own timetable. There will be many planning sessions and shopping trips between now and August. This being the first grandchild, it will be very hard to control the emotions and excitement. By the way, Grandpa predicts a boy!

Morris Document 24

Help the Children

It was January 1999, a cold Sunday morning around five thirty. Suddenly a loud noise woke me up. I rose up straight in my bed. I looked at my wife; she was sound asleep beside me. I jumped from my bed. I must see what had hit my house. I raced up the hallway. I glanced in my daughter's room; she too was fast asleep. Even the dog was asleep. As I entered the kitchen, I heard this voice, not an audible voice, but one that was inside me say, "Help the children."

But I must find what had hit my house. I raced out into the backyard. There was six inches of snow on the ground, and there I stood barefoot in my underwear. It was then I thought I was losing my mind. I went back inside and dried my feet. I told myself I was having a bad dream and decided to go back to bed. I crawled into my bed to get warm and forget what had just happened. It was then I became deathly sick at my stomach. I remember walking up the hallway to get on the couch. That was when I heard it again, "Help the children." It came two more times that morning. I then decided it was God telling me to go back to college to become a teacher. When Monday came, I was on my way to my old high school to talk to my old principal to learn what I needed to do to become a teacher. As I told him what had happened that led me to him, he just sat there smiling, with his fingertips together. You see, he knew all about the voice I had been talking about. He told me what I needed to know, and I was on my way. About halfway home, reality sunk in. I was unemployed with two kids in college. My wife was struggling to make ends meet. How could I go to college? So I tossed the idea out the window.

I now wanted to step back to October the previous year. I had taken a test for the prison system, mainly because my wife had wanted me to; we needed some income. So I took the test to appease her and forgot about it. We now move ahead to March 1999. I was working as a janitor at the VA hospital in Marion, Illinois. This was the most satisfying job I have ever had. I had the opportunity to visit with these old vets and listen to their stories. I couldn't wait to get to work each day. I worked evening shift. One night I got home, and my wife told me a Debbie Bishop had called from the Vienna prison. My heart sank. I thought, "Not now. I'm satisfied with the job I have." But I told my wife I would call the next day. Debbie answered the phone. I told her who I was. She then offered me a job at the Vienna prison. I told her I didn't want to work at a prison. She said, "Excuse me?" Again I told her I didn't want to work at a prison. I then told her I would check with the VA hospital to see if I could get on full-time. She agreed to call me back the next day. She called me the next day to offer me this job; my answer was the same. She then told me I had scored the highest score on the test. I said, "Sure I did." She said I really had scored the highest score. Before I mislead you on this score, I must tell you how the scoring system works. You have your basic score plus work experience (I had twenty years) plus military time (I had four years) plus supervisory skills. Add all this up and you can see how I had such a high score. I then told Ms. Bishop if I have such a high score, find me a job. I don't want to work at the Vienna prison. She told me she would call me back the next day. Her call came the third day. She asked me if I would take a job at the Dixon Springs Boot Camp. I told her I didn't know they had a boot camp and asked her to tell me about it. She said it housed children from seventeen to thirty-five. HELP THE CHILDREN. I told her I would take the job. She didn't know what to say. I know why I am working at the boot camp; this is where I belong. I have always had a burden for children. Maybe it's because I am still a kid at heart, who knows!

Morris Document 25

Our Storms

It was 6:00 a.m. on Friday in early October. I had risen early as I did most mornings. This was my quiet time, the time that I did my best thinking and felt close to God. As I stepped out of the garage and took my first breath of that crisp morning, I noticed the moon was about to set in the west. I suddenly found my mind sent back to my days in the navy. For you see, I would be on the fantail of my ship each night while we were at sea to watch that same moon sink into the ocean. In turn I would watch the sun rise from the ocean in the morning. These were the times I would be at peace; it was quiet and tranquil. I would think of my girlfriend and parents and home. At sea you are exposed to encounter many storms, much like in our lives. A night I will always remember was the worst storms of the sea I have ever endured. We had been on the North Atlantic when our boilers failed. We were dead in the water off the coast of Scotland. We were finally towed into Faslane, Scotland, and anchored in the harbor. For three months we sat there waiting word on what they would do with us. The people in Scotland were warm and friendly; they made us feel welcome. We found we were to either go to the dry docks in South Hampton, England, or be towed across the choppy North Atlantic. Soon word came that we would be towed. I was among the skeleton crew that would make this journey. The tug would take thirty-five to forty-five days to pull us that 3,800-plus-mile trip. About a week into the tow, word came of a typhoon forming at sea, but they said we would be clear of its path. By 4:00 p.m. that afternoon, it was clear they had been very wrong; the seas were getting rough very quickly. By 5:00 p.m. they ordered all watertight doors closed, and no one was to be on the main deck. By 7:00 p.m. we were in heavy seas, and we were taking thirty-degree rolls. I was to have the midwatch that night, which meant I went on watch at midnight and continued till 4:00 a.m. At 8:00 p.m. I decided to get into my bottom rack and get some sleep. By 9:00 p.m. I had been thrown from my rack three times. I decided to go to the log room and check the clinometer to see how much we were listing. It was up to forty degrees by this time. You could barely walk up the passageways or keep your trays on the table in the mess decks. At midnight I assumed my watch. My watch consisted of carrying a .45-caliber pistol with two clips and a sounding tape. This tape was used to check the lower decks to check for water, which would mean there were leaks. My first two hours were uneventful; the seas were even rougher. At 2:00 a.m. I went to the bridge to report there was no damage. As I passed behind this huge black man on the helm, he said, "Tow broke." As I looked off the bow, I noticed the bright light of the tug was gone. It then dawned on me that the towline was severed. I can't begin to describe the horror I felt at that moment. I thought of my girlfriend and my parents. Would I ever see them again? As these thoughts began to flood my mind, my eyes shifted to my far left. I then saw a glow in that terrible storm. It was the stern of the tug. Suddenly my fears were replaced with hope. None of us slept the rest of that terrible night, but that morning we watched as the sea began to calm, and out of it came a wonderful, bright sun. What a welcomed sight for a bunch of scared, homesick sailors. We were attached to the tug and continued on our journey home.

    This story didn't have any real meaning to me then; it was just another page in my past. Until seventeen years later, one of my daughters was having some problems in college. I went to her in hopes I could talk to her and calm her fears. I relayed to her the story you have just read. I went on to tell her that our storms in life are much like the storms at sea, that they are usually short-lived and the sun would come up on a new day. Sometimes our storms rage on till we think we will never survive, but eventually, they subside, and we continue on our journey. That night in the North Atlantic, we lost our tow. It wasn't the tug's fault; it was us that lost our grip. It was then I wondered how many times I have lost the grip on the rope in my life. I learned another important lesson that night, a lesson that would take many storms in my life to realize—that the rope I refer to is God, that when my most rough times have come in my life, these are the times I have turned loose of the rope; that as long as I have a good grip on the rope, I can weather any storm. So as I view storms, I have a different light now. My storms seem very trivial at times now for I know all I have to do is pay attention to what's around me and spend some early-morning looking at the moon and sun.

Morris Document 26

The Day I Hooked Up with Little Elvis

It was Saturday, March 26, 1977. It was an unusually warm spring in Southern Illinois. I had just finished my midnight shift at the coal mine. I had brought my fishing equipment with me, with plans of going fishing this morning. As I arrived at the pond, I could see fish working the water. I felt it would be a great day to fish. I cast out two rods to fish for catfish. I then started to reach for my bass rod, but as I started to grab it, I saw a large wave on the other side of the pond. I started to get my tackle box but opted instead to take one extra plug, which I attached to the loose end of my belt. I started to ease around the pond to get into position. I cast my first cast, and as soon as it hit the water, there was a big explosion of water as the large bass ate my bait. I leaned down to reel the slack line up, then I jerked back with my pole and body to set the hook. As I did, instant pain shot into my Little Elvis. I can't remember pain that intense, but I fought to land the fish. A big fish will wear down pretty quick; this one was no exception. As I landed the fish, I grabbed him by the lower lip and tossed him behind me, threw my rod to the side, and began to remove the other hook. Luckily, the hook hadn't gotten as deep as the barb, but it was deep enough it left a scar I still have to this day. After removing the hook, I turned to look at the fish. It would turn out to be a nine-pound bass, the largest bass I had ever caught. I got so excited that I ran right past the other rods I had set out and went straight to my father-in-law's house to weigh the fish.

Some days later, after freezing the fish, I took the fish to Fred Washburn, a taxidermist in Carterville, Illinois, to have it mounted. He asked what the fishing story was behind this fish, so I told him the story you have just read. As he wiped the tears from his eyes, he said, "I have heard all kinds of fishing stories, but I've never heard that one. It has to be the truth. But I have to ask, why did you worry more about the fish than you did Little Elvis?"

I said, "The answer is simple. I knew what I had on that plug was much bigger than what I had on the other one! A true story, I have the scar to prove it!"

Morris Document 27

Passions from the Past

It's 4:30 a.m.; my peaceful sleep has been disturbed by the sound of thunder from the west. Soon the bright flashes of lightning illuminate my bedroom till I can no longer sleep, and I sit up in my bed, wide awake. A few minutes pass before I can hear light pecks of raindrops hitting my windows. Soon the lights pecks are replaced by hard torrents and sheets of rain that now pound my roof.

It's early June in Southern Illinois; it has been an unusually dry spring. The farmers have plowed and tilled there land; all they need is the much-needed rain to moisten this rich soil before they plant their crops for the year. My father owns a 320-acre farm. It is now rented out and farmed by someone else since my father has retired. As a kid I helped my father farm these fields. I know the ground well. This particular morning is the morning I have waited for all winter; it is the morning the fields are worked up and a hard rain has soaked and washed the dirt away to expose the tools of an ancient past. As you may have guessed by now, I am an Indian artifact collector. My passions from the past have been revived this early morning.

As I stir around in my dark bedroom, I gather my clothes and try to be quiet to not wake my wife. As I pass up the hallway, I quickly glance into my daughter's room; she too is fast asleep. As I go into the kitchen, I grab a quick bite and slip out the back door and take my first breath of the new day. By now it's 5:30 a.m. The sun has lit up the gentle countryside. I gaze to the east. I can see the ridges that are drenched with rain. The soil seems so much darker than the rest of the field. I walk the mere quarter of a mile and take my first glance at the ground I have waited all winter to see. Before me I can see chips of flint. They shine in the morning sun. I can feel it will be a good day. After a few more minutes, I find the tip of an arrowhead. I clean the mud off it and slide it into my back pocket. After a few more minutes, I see a white tip protruding out of the ground at an angle. As I bend over, I cautiously pick it up; it is a small St. Charles dovetail, seemingly undamaged. This one piece has made the mud and lack of sleep well worthwhile. As the hours pass that day, I had found seven broken points and eight complete pieces, along with the broken tip of a hatchet.

My passions have been stirred deeply this morning. As I stood there in the mud on this ridge this morning, I couldn't help but think of these ancient inhabitants of this land. What were they like? How long were they here, and what made them leave? That particular day, I did something I have done many times in the forty-plus years I've roamed these lands. I closed my eyes and took a trip into the past. As I closed my eyes, I could smell the campfires and see women around them, preparing the food their family would eat that day. I could see children running wildly through the camp, playing with a pretend bow and arrow. In the distance I could hear the sound of someone chipping flint to make the points either to kill the game they would eat or to protect his family. In my vision, I glanced at the creek nearby. I noticed how clear it seemed. Absent were garbage and chemicals, and the water was so clear you could see the fish swimming. As I looked back to the west, there were no power lines, no roads, and no airplanes overhead. There were no tractors or fences, only quiet. Around me were only green forests and gentle plains and quiet people that took care of the land and the land in turn took care of them. As I opened my eyes, I realized my journey had come to an end.

Over the years, I have taken this journey countless times. I have walked hundreds of miles in these fields in quest of my passion; I have never left unsatisfied. I have taught my children this simple hobby, in hopes they too would share my passions. I hope to someday have grandchildren that will take me by the finger and let me lead them to these passionate places of our ancient past.

Morris Document 28

A Chance Meeting?

I have always been the type to question everything. As far back as I can remember, I would wonder why things happen as they do. I would never be satisfied with the answer that it was just a coincidence. I could accept the answer "It was just meant to be." I could not count the many times I have run into someone I had had on my mind, or an old friend that I hadn't seen in a long time, and later would think how strange our meeting was. It wasn't strange at all; it was meant to be. Was our meeting a chance meeting or simply meant to be? I feel all things happen for a reason; this is the way I choose to live my life.

Today, I decided to stop on my way to work and get a Subway sandwich. I was in uniform, standing in line. I noticed this man ahead of me kept looking at me. Finally, he turned and asked me where I worked. I told him, then he returned to his place in line. After a minute or so, he turned to me and said, "How can you stand to work with the scum of the earth?" I told him I didn't look at them that way. Again he turned and walked away. I ate my sandwich and started to leave. This same man waved at me and said, "Have a nice shift." I hit the road with this chance meeting on my mind. What did it mean? As I drove, I started to think about what he said: the scum of the earth. Granted, these inmates had made mistakes to get them where they were at, but most of them would admit to their mistakes and accept their punishment. At this point, it came so clear to me what this whole thing was about. This was not a chance meeting at all; it was meant to show me that the scum, as he called it, are not always whom we think they are. We, the ones on the outside, have to take some credit for some of the scum, the ones who appear so holy and never admit to wrongdoing or making mistakes. The only difference in the two is they got caught.

As I look back over my fifty-three years on this earth, I have had many encounters that I couldn't explain. Many of them I can now see in a different light. I can at last begin to see what they had taught me. I now try to live my life looking for what these chance meetings are trying to teach me. Was it a chance meeting? I don't think so!

Morris Document 29

They Called Him Noah

Noah 5 yrs.

Seldom in our lives on earth does something come along that transforms us and changes our lives forever. Other than becoming a Christian, the event that changed me forever was the birth of our first grandchild, a boy; they call him Noah. While rushing to St. Louis, my oldest daughter gave birth to a son. I wanted so bad to be there for this event, but when it was time for it to arrive, it was time. From the first time I was able to see him, I felt we would be good friends. He was a bit small with red hair; he was perfect. As the days went by, I would rock him and talk to him. Little did I know a bond was being formed that would last a lifetime. The Christmas of 2003 was in full swing. I was in Walmart, doing some last-minute shopping, when my cell phone rang. It was my wife. She told me of a call she had gotten from our daughter in Maryville. She had told her mother she had a big surprise for her at Christmas. My wife asked me what I thought. I simply said, "She's pregnant." We talked some more when I got home and laughed at the thought of being grandparents. We even went to our workplaces and told everyone we were going to be grandparents. So we went on toward Christmas with the excitement of the big surprise from our daughter and son-in-law. Christmas came, and our daughter called as they drove to our home. She asked if everyone was there and if they were up yet. They finally arrived and began to bring presents in. It was finally time to unwrap the gifts. At last my daughter got up and handed my wife a gift and said, "Mom, here is your big surprise."

My wife stared at her in disbelief and said, "This is my big surprise? I thought you were pregnant."

My daughter looked at her and said, "Who said I was pregnant?"

We all had a big laugh as we finished unwrapping gifts that day.

On we go to New Year's Day. We had taken our middle daughter to St. Louis for a flight to Texas. We were to stop by our other daughter's to eat ham and beans to bring us good luck for the coming year. My son-in-law met us at the door and told us our daughter was fixing her hair and would be out soon. Finally, she arrived at the table, sat down, and said, "I'm really pregnant this time," and began to cry for joy. My wife and I sat there somewhat stunned. You see, she had been pregnant at Christmas, but none knew it. You see, God doesn't always work on our time schedule as we think he should; he does things his way. After a long, hot summer, she gave birth to this little giant on July 29. He has brought so much joy to this family since joining us, joy to the level I never thought possible. His smile lights up a room, and his laughter can soften a hardened heart—he is my grandson. I dream of the day we can do things together and I can show him the many wonders of this world. I only hope I can be a mentor and role model to him, for we already have a strong bond to work with. I never thought I could love a child as much as I do this grandson of mine. I loved my own three daughters very much. For some reason, a grandchild is different; it is a love that makes you do crazy things. When Noah was two days old, I went to Rural King to get him a cast iron tractor. As I looked at them, my eyes shifted to a Radio Flyer coaster wagon with wooden sides. I went to look at it, and I was hooked, but I didn't stop there. I ended up buying the wagon, a pup wagon to pull behind, a Radio Flyer tricycle, as well as a Radio Flyer wheel barrow. I thought that this was so crazy but bought them anyway. So I guess you have gathered by now how important this little guy is to me; he is my grandson. They called him Noah!

Morris Document 30

My First Granddaughter

Every grandpa dreams of grandchildren. I am no different. We already have one grandson, and now we longed for a granddaughter. Along comes May 29, 2009, and along comes the most beautiful little girl I had ever seen. Her big eyes and black hair broke my heart. Her grandma cried, for as I had a wonderful grandson, now she had a granddaughter. Her eyes and smile can light up the dimmest room and soften the hardest heart. As the months went by, her dark hair became the blondest blond one has ever seen. She looks just like her mother as her mother looks just like my wife, so you can see I have three beautiful women in my life, along with my grandson, who is the boy I never had. Only rarely in life does something come along that transforms you and makes tears come to your eyes—she has accomplished this feat. She has brought so much joy to our family, and now she walks and talks and is very healthy. She is so special to us all, and I never realized how much fun she is. We loved our own three daughters very much, but grandchildren are a totally different type of love. I love her so much for she is special; she's my granddaughter! Her name is Halle.

Morris Document 31

The Fields Were Muddy

Early one morning, I arose in the darkness as I usually do every morning to witness the sunrise. As the sun lit up the gentle countryside, I began to notice the harvest had only been partially harvested because the rains had come and it became muddy. The ruts they had made were filled with rainwater. As I stood there and looked in that morning light, I began to think of the meaning God was trying to show me. The harvest was ripe, and I knew the fields would have to become solid again before they could harvest what remained. Again I wondered what he was trying to tell me. It was then that the meaning he was trying to reveal to me about the muddy fields became so clear to me. I began to think of my life and how the mud I had allowed to come into my life had kept me from enjoying the richness of the harvest God had intended me to reap. The greed I had let myself view as so important I thought enter my life that had consumed me to the point I had forgotten what was really important in life and blinded me to the point I had no real purpose. I was so busy with this greed that I had neglected my family and friends and was wrapped up in the things of this world, and I no longer had a clear view of reality of the things I now see as really important to me. In the darkness I thought of how many times as a child I had been scared. I thought how the darkness was evil because I had been told things of the night were scary and been told to fear them. As the sun cracked the eastern sky, I began to notice the birds began to chirp as if to tell me the safety of the sun had allowed them to feel secure. They were no

SUNRISE

longer afraid of the predators that sought them in the darkness. As I witnessed this, I thought of those predators of the night we face, like the thieves that would steal from us or the murderers that would take our lives and the ones that do sinful things in the cover of the darkness, only to be revealed in the light of day. The light I refer to is Jesus Christ, for he supplies the light that shows us the way. Through him, our vision is no longer clouded or muddy, for he has perfect vision. Many times we allow our vision to become obscured by the many things of the world that at times cause us to be blinded to the point we totally lose our vision and sight. As I stumbled along the wide path. I bumped into many obstacles along the way because I viewed things and people and thought this was normal, when in fact this was not normal at all. I can now see the wonder of the world I live in and can see how blind I really was, all because of the rising of the sun. I now think we all experience our own muddy fields in life that we trudge through as we weigh ourselves down with the mud we collect in life. I must wait till my field gets solid before I try to finish the harvest in my life. For me, I had to experience the sunrise before my vision cleared, and I felt the weight of the mud weighing me down was lifted.

Morris Document 32

Her Name Was Kelly

My story begins in 1995, on a darkened softball field in Marion, Illinois. My team of nine- and ten-year-olds have won their softball game. I have turned the lights off, and the last little girl had been picked up by her parents. You would be surprised how many children were dropped off at these games. The parent would leave and not attend the game that the child wanted them to watch, only to show up two hours later to pick them up. I cannot begin to count the times the parents would show up smelling like alcohol.

One night, when everyone was gone, the lights were off, and my equipment was in my truck, I lit that cigarette I thought I deserved after that tight game. I had only taken a few puffs from that cigarette when my world exploded. From out of the darkness came this innocent voice that pierced the night. She said one sentence to me: "Why do you do that?" I could not move or speak. I finally regained my composure enough to say, "I know this is a bad habit. I need to quit." You see, I was a closet smoker. I would only smoke when I thought there wasn't anyone around. You see, a coach is not only a coach; he should also be a role model for the young ladies. In the eyes of this nine-year-old, she thought I did no wrong. She had these dark eyes that could pierce you as she gazed at you, and when she would smile, there were these large dimples that would make you smile. That night there were no dimples, only those dark eyes that demanded an answer. I had no answer because I had no defense. She lived real close to the ball field and had seen my lights and came over to tell me how much she wanted to be on my team because we seemed to have so much fun as we played. She would go on to be on my team as they chose All Stars. I would go on to be chosen the coach of the team. Our team would win our tournament in the Northern Zone and be invited to the nationals in the east. This girl would end up riding part of the way with my wife and my daughter to Sterling, West Virginia, to attend the national finals in softball for girls in the nine- to ten-year-old bracket. We would end up placing fifth in the nation, not too bad for a group of girls from deep Southern Illinois.

As I tell this story, I can't help but think of my own three daughters and wonder how many times I had failed to be their role model. You see that when we think the darkness will hide the things we all do, there is someone always watching, but they may choose to be silent. This same girl is now a beautiful young woman who attends a major college in the South on a softball scholarship, and I am very happy to have been a part of her life. If people aren't watching us, God always is; you can't hide anything from him.

As I told this story, one comes to mind that is as powerful as the one you have just read and is along the same lines. It involves my own daughter. She and I, on a Sunday, were sent by my wife to get some things for a Sunday cookout. As we entered this large grocery store, people were everywhere. Our path that day led us down the left side of a huge salad bar. On this salad bar was a huge container of black olives. I love black olives, so as we passed, I grabbed one and crammed it in my mouth. My beautiful eight-year-old was directly behind me. About halfway down the aisle, my daughter hit me with such force I thought she used a sledge hammer. She said these words: "Dad, you're not setting a very good example for me." My world exploded. For you see, I had just taught my precious daughter that it was okay to steal. "Dad did it, and Dad is my role model." Whether it is taking a black olive or robbing a bank, stealing is stealing. As I whirled around in the middle of that aisle, I looked directly into the innocent eyes of my daughter. She was laughing as if it wasn't a big deal. She taught me another important lesson as Kelley had, that someone is always watching us on this journey we call life, that we aren't as smart as we sometimes think we are. I can think of many lessons children have taught me as my wife and I have raised three beautiful daughters, some we choose to learn from, some we choose to ignore. I now have a wonderful grandson. I only hope I can show him the way. We all fail along the way at times. Sometimes we simply need to listen to that quiet voice we all hear that is inside us all at times. The only time we can't hear this voice is when we choose not to listen.

Morris Document 33

His Passions

December 19, 2003

In April 2000, a friend of mine named Becky Fosse called me to ask me if I would help her clean out an old garage prior to a yard sale she was having. I told her I would and drove to her home in Whiteash, Illinois. Upon arrival, she told me to help her price what items I could and that if I found anything I wanted, to simply take it. After doing as I was told, I looked on a sidewall and saw a wooden box. In this box I saw an old duck call inside. This old duck call and a small set of scales were what I told her I would like to have, and she agreed. I went home that night and showed the duck call to my wife and told her I thought it was very old and, to the right person, would be very valuable. She seemed not to be as sure as I was. The years went by, and I was still in search of the collector I felt was out there somewhere. In the year 2002, I attended the John A. Logan Hunting and Fishing Days. It was on a Sunday; I went in hope of finding this collector I was in search of. One of the vendors looked at my call and told me to follow him into the auditorium to one of the guys that was a judge of the duck-calling contest. I showed him this call. His eyes lit up as he held it in his hand, but he wasn't the person I sought. But he gave me a name I could contact who might have some information I could use. That name was Harvey Pitts, a decoy collector from Du Quoin, Illinois. He in turn gave me the name of a man who lived near Hornbeak, Tennessee; this man was named Russell Caldwell. I wrote Mr. Caldwell and enclosed some pictures of the duck call and told him to contact me if he was interested. One day I received a phone call from Mr. Caldwell to inform me he was very interested in this duck call I possessed. He went on to ask me if I had any passions. I had never had anyone ask me such a question, so he explained. He went on to explain he had a passion for collecting duck calls for many years, because his most precious moments involved hunting with his friends and sons. He went on to tell me one of his sons had fallen victim to a disease and felt he would lose him soon. He asked me if I would drive to Union City, Tennessee, and meet him; he even offered to pay for my gas. After a brief moment, I agreed to attend this meeting. We set up a date and hung up.

The day finally came for this meeting; I drove to Union City and arrived within ten minutes of the agreed time. As I pulled into the parking space, I saw a large man in a camouflaged hunting coat, waving to me as I got out of my truck. I entered McDonald's and met a new friend. We introduced ourselves to each other; he offered to buy me a cup of coffee. Before I left to get the coffee, I handed Mr. Caldwell the old duck call. As I was walking away, I couldn't help but notice the expression on the face of this huge man. It was the look of sheer delight that a father has when he holds his firstborn child. When I came back to the table, Mr. Caldwell asked me if he could take the call apart. I said it was okay. I never knew it would come apart if it hadn't been for a young man I work with named Tom Quertermous. The day he took it apart, I thought he had broken it. As we shared with each other that day, I soon began to see what Mr. Caldwell meant about his passions. He asked me where my passion lay; I told him I was an Indian artifact collector. I soon began to understand what he meant by passions, and I realized really for the first time in the forty-two years of collecting arrowheads that I too had a passion. He was very interested in the story that was behind this old duck call. The story I told is the account you have just read. He wanted to know where it had been since I had found it. I told him it had laid on my mantel for over two years. Mr. Caldwell at that point shared a story with me that touched my very soul. He said he had to constantly tend to his son, that some of his body functions were shutting down. That very morning he was preparing to leave to meet me, his son had reached out to grab his arm and asked him where he was going. He replied, "I am going to meet a man who has a duck call I may be interested in." His son replied, "Dad, I would be honored to buy the call for you. That would be my Christmas present to you." As I sat there in a McDonald's in Union City, Tennessee, in front of a stranger I had just met, I again began to see another passion he had, that for his family. You see, Mr. Caldwell had shared this passion with this son he was losing. It was all I could do to sit there that morning. My emotions almost took over, but suddenly I began to understand what had brought us together. I was simply a messenger; I was the guy with a duck call. The son wanted to do something special for his dad. The dad wanted to see his sick son happy. But I really feel I got the blessing this day, because I saw happiness on the face of a man that also showed pain for a son he was about to lose. I went on to tell him everything I knew of this call. What I didn't tell him was that I had blown the call on my way to meet him that day. What a chuckle he would have gotten.

Present also that day was Mr. Caldwell's lifelong friend and collector. They acted like two kids as they gaped over this old call. Mr. Caldwell purchased that call that cool day in December; he asked me if I was satisfied. I said I was, but my satisfaction was far more than monetary. You see, I did exactly what I had wanted to do with this duck call. I had put it into the hands of a man who truly had a deep passion for the art and history behind this seemingly insignificant piece of wood. We shook hands. I got into my truck and drove away so fulfilled I could hardly keep my truck between the ditches. I told Mr. Caldwell that day that I had made a new friend and that I felt that God had put us on a collision course to meet this day. I also told him that I believed that a stranger was just a friend we hadn't met yet. As I hit the interstate that day, I felt a little guilty—guilty because I had taken money for something that had given me so much satisfaction. The joy he had expressed as he held that old duck call made me feel very good. I hope someday to cross paths with Mr. Russell Caldwell again. He is the person who shared with me the meaning of his passions and also made me aware of my own!

Morris Document 34

The Seeds and the Hatchet

When I was a young man of twelve, I would sell seeds every spring. This particular spring was no different from the previous springs, for I would pedal my bicycle even in the snow to sell the seeds that would earn me this great prize. As I look back, I was suckered, for the prizes were no way worth the hours and pedaling I had invested. Every year without fail in my seed order, they would send me the normal seeds—tomatoes, corn, peas, and some flowers—and they never failed to also send me okra. If you know anything about okra, you and I know that no one buys this stuff. So every year it would lie there in the bottom of the box like the last kid to be chosen for a grade-school ball team. But I was lucky. I had this old couple that lived at the end of a long driveway that was lined by many large oak trees, and they would always take it off my hands. I made sure there was good light of day when I pedaled my bike down this road, because it gave me the creeps to be there when it was dark. Every year they would buy these packets of okra seed, and I never could figure out why. As I became older, I now see that they were lonely; they simply wanted company. This particular spring, my prize had been a small hatchet and leather case that went on my belt. I was very proud of this hatchet and wore it everywhere I went. One day Mom sent me down to the hog floor to get my older brother for dinner. At twelve, a kid is getting to the age where he seems to want to cuss a bit. I was no different. That day as I approached the hog floor, I found him with a shovel, scooping hog waste from the floor. I thought, "Boy, he must have done something really bad, because this was without question the worst job on the farm." As I got there, I cussed him and told him it was dinnertime, to get his ass up to the house. I knew he couldn't run, so I had a head start. I could be safe with Mom before he would get to the house. About halfway to the house, this devious thought came to me. I would find a small block of wood, embed my hatchet in it, unbutton my shirt, lay the wood on my chest, then button my shirt up and make it appear someone had killed me with this hatchet. As I lay there, I thought of the look on my brother's face when he saw this one. It would have to be the best stunt either of us had done. All of a sudden, I heard this bloodcurdling scream from the house side. It was my poor mother; she thought my brother had killed me. I could not get up fast enough to get a head start on Mom. She got me before I could even get away, for I knew I had had it. She slapped me with her hands and beat me with her fists, and I deserved every bit of it. As I looked toward the barn, I could see my brother laughing at me, and I too saw the humor he must have seen. He knew as I did that this was one of my stunts that had indeed backfired on me. When I look back on things like this, I wonder how we survived during these years on the farm. I guess it was from the laughter we enjoyed from all the stunts, and there was plenty of them to laugh at. Boy, those other boys sure pulled a lot of stunts. I was usually the victim—*not*.

Morris Document 35

Just an Old Duck Call

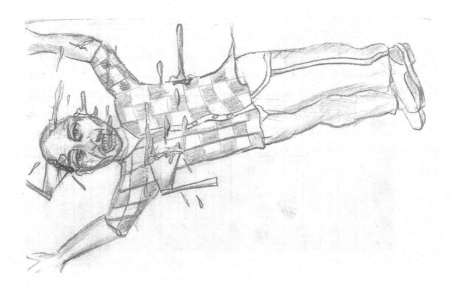

He gazed at the old duck call in his hand like a father would gaze into the eyes of his firstborn child as he held it for the first time. This was a gaze I saw on the face of a great man I met one winter morning in Union City, Tennessee. I had been put in touch with this man by a man named Harvey Pitts. As we talked about this call, I began to see his true passion for this seemingly unimportant piece of wood I possessed. I sold that call to him that cold, crisp morning in December. It was then that he shared with me why he couldn't make the journey to my hometown. You see, he had a son with whom he had duck-hunted since the boy was very young. His most precious memories centered around the times they had spent duck hunting on Reelfoot Lake. He told me his son had fallen deathly ill, and he felt he would lose him soon. As I sat there in Union City, Tennessee, with a man I had just met, I began to feel my emotions rise. I thought I would have to go to the restroom so he wouldn't see me cry. For you see, I not only saw through his eyes the passion of this man for duck calls. I also saw the pain in his eyes as he talked about this son. I knew at that moment I had met a great man as well as a new friend. That very morning, as he was leaving for our meeting, his son had asked him where he was going. He told him he was going to meet a man that had a duck call he would like to own. His son told him he would be honored to buy that call for him; it would be his Christmas present for him. The touched me deeply. It was then that it became clear to me why I was there. You see, I was just a messenger. I was the guy that had the duck call. The father was trying to care for his son who had accompanied him on so many hunts, and the son was trying to pay his dad back for all the good times he had provided him. As I looked at him, I realized our meeting wasn't a chance meeting at all, that the whole matter of me finding that call all the way to my journey to Union City had all been arranged. All things happen for a reason. Mr. Caldwell would lose his son in the spring of the following year. I know that was painful for him as well as the rest of his family. As for me, I feel I got the blessing that cold day in December. I was honored to have been part of his life he shared with me. I hit the interstate that day with mixed feelings. I knew I just witnessed something great, but I also felt guilty because I had taken money for something that had blessed me so much. Someday I hope to cross paths with this man again. He is the one who shared his passions with me and made me understand passions in a new light.

Morris Document 36

The Dummy

The year was 1982. I worked in a large strip mine in the heart of Southern Illinois. Coal miners are a special breed of men and are known for their great sense of humor. Not a day goes by, it seems, that you do not hear of or see a funny story. It was mid-July. I had just started my shift as a welder. I saw this older man coming toward me with a small box in his hands. As he stopped, he looked around to make sure no one heard our conversation then started to tell of the contents of the box. He said, "Do you remember how old Joe's bottom lip hangs down when he gets mad?" I said I did. He then pulled the ventriloquist dummy from the box. I began to laugh so hard I thought I would wet myself. For that dummy's bottom lip looked just like Joe's. He gave me the box and said, "I thought you might know what to do with this." I began to think how I could get this to Joe without being detected. As I looked at the box, I noticed the man's name had been removed. The wheels in my head began to spin. I took the box to the warehouse and asked Gary if he wanted to get involved in a small sting operation. After I told him whom we were going to sting, he was eager to help. He put an old UPS label on the box and wrote Joe's name and my location. I told him to call Joe's boss and tell him Joe has a package in the warehouse. His boss came and got the package and took it to Joe's workplace. He gave the package to Joe, and he began to open it. As he reached into the box and pulled the dummy out, he immediately crammed it back in the box with that lip hanging out even farther. He would not find out until years later who had started this stunt and who were involved in the steps that made this stunt work. But there is more to this story.

The year 1982 was also the year of the world's fair in Knoxville, Tennessee. Joe had told me he was going to the fair; he even told me where he was staying. Big mistake. Again the wheels in my head began to spin. Remember, we coal miners enjoy our fun. So I called down to Knoxville and asked if Joe was staying there. He was, so I asked to be connected to his room. Joe answered the phone. I told him I was the manager of the motel and had a favor to ask of him. I told him our band had canceled for tonight, and I was wondering if he would put on a puppet show in the lounge. I could feel the heat coming through the phone as he cussed me. He asked, "Who is this?" I told him, and he asked how on earth I found him. I told him that he had told me where he was staying. It was then he began to laugh, a laugh I had not heard in a long time. He told me I would have to pay for this one. I told him whatever the price, I would pay.

This is just one of the many stories I have from my days as a coal miner. The mine is closed now. I now work in a boot camp. I miss the good times we had, and I can see a new set of stories to tell. Laughter is truly the best medicine. We have to break the boredom and make our journey on this earth much more enjoyable.

Morris Document 37

The Trolling Motor

One afternoon my younger brother and I went fishing at a mine lake near where I worked. The day's fishing had been very good, and we were enjoying each other's company. The lake was notorious for large bass, and we had caught our share that day. We usually got together as much as we could, and I had introduced him to this great hole of water. The last time we had been there, he had gotten us stuck. I had ended up walking two miles to get help while he fished. So this particular day, I had vowed to outfish him. Our day had been great as we talked and laughed. As we went around the bank, I noticed a small water snake coiled in a small bush on the bank. I commented on how pretty the snake was, when my brother jumped as he saw it. It was then I thought of a way to have some fun at his expense. I turned my boat ninety degrees and slowly moved out into the lake. I then put the motor in reverse on low and began to back into the bank. He asked me what I was doing. I then told him the motor was stuck and I would have to work on it. The closer we got to the snake, the more nervous he got. Finally, he was within five feet of the snake. Suddenly I felt my boat begin to tip. As I looked back, I saw my brother coming up the side of the boat with a boat paddle in his hand. He stated, "If you didn't have the truck keys in your pocket, I would boat paddle your ass." The rest of the day was filled with laughter as we fished. To this day, I still kid him about this great, adventurous day we shared on the pristine lake that day.

Morris Document 38

Letter

Sunday, November 12, 2006

Russell,

As my dad and I was looking at the book this morning that you sent me, I was showing him the picture of the old call you bought. I began to think about our meeting that cold morning in December when we first met. He asked me what I had got for it. I told him $800, and his eyes rolled in disbelief. I then told him it wasn't the value in terms of dollars that satisfied me, that there is more in life than money. First of all, you made me aware of the passions that I possess that I was somewhat unaware I had. The passion I had that I let go by the wayside was my deep passion for God. I had let this passion slip in my busy life. This was one that is very important to me and could not be replaced by things of this world. Even artifact collecting could not measure up to the satisfaction of having Jesus Christ. I am the one who gained from our meeting this cold morning, for I gained a friend for life that I never would have gotten if not for that duck call I had found in that old garage two years prior. The blessings will never go away, unlike money. Through you and your son, I was shown a passion you had for your family that in turn made me aware of the passion I possessed for my own family. I feel as though I owe you for these things. This is why I felt guilty as I drove away that morning, for I knew you had given me much more than I had given me. I feel that all things happen for a reason, that by finding that old call, the Lord was guiding me on the path that caused us to meet. I would have to put this meeting's importance right up there with meeting God and the meeting of my wife. So I was the winner in this race. In life's journey, we have many opportunities. These opportunities can pass us by if we don't pay close attention and notice what is really important for our lives. Our meeting made me more aware of the opportunities in my life that I would have let pass if not for that seemingly insignificant piece of wood. I thank God I met you that cold December morning in Union City. This meeting opened my eyes to a wonderful world that I had somewhat forgotten. I am proud to have you as a friend. Your wonderful books made me aware of the many treasures I have in life, especially the story about Chester that mirrored the relationship I have with my own dad. I hope someday to see you again, but not here on earth. I'll see you in heaven.

Morris Document 39

Letter

December 11, 2002

Mr. Caldwell,

After our meeting today, I felt compelled to sit down and express to you how much I enjoyed the day. I felt as though I have known you for years. You remind me of my father, as far as how easy you are to talk to. Your children are very fortunate to have you as their father.

After I drove home, I couldn't keep my mind off the look on your face as you cuddled that duck call. You reminded me of a father as he held his firstborn child; your passion you spoke of was magnified from your face! I felt a deep sense of fulfillment in knowing I had in some small way contributed in filling your passion. I now am confident the call is in its rightful place. I have felt all along it needed to be in the hands of a serious collector such as yourself. As I drove down the interstate, I had a sense of guilt as far as getting paid for something that gave me so much pleasure. The money was fine, but dollars have nothing to do with fulfillment!

Hopefully, someday our paths will cross again. They say a stranger is just a friend we haven't met yet; that surely was the case today. Mr. Pitts told me you were an honest man. I feel he gave me some accurate information. The Lord put us three on a collision course; it has certainly been my pleasure. If I can ever be of service to you, please feel free to contact me.

Thank you,

Rodger Morris
9391 Saraville Rd.
Marion, IL 62959

Morris Document 40

Put Me in, Coach, I'm Ready to Play

As far back as I can remember, I have had a special concern for children. Whether it was my own three daughters or that cute baby in the grocery store, I found myself attached. I believe this concern came from my uncle Duke. He always was interested in what I did at school or in sports; he always had the time to listen. I felt good in knowing he cared. He'd drop whatever he was doing to take time for me. This is not to say that my parents didn't; they did. My dad worked and farmed to raise four sons, and he was very busy. I feel my uncle is where I got my interest in taking time for children. I felt this way all through my school years. After high school, I enlisted in the US Navy and left home for the first time. After my schools, I was assigned to a ship in Charleston, South Carolina. I advanced quickly and was soon in charge of a repair shop with eight people to supervise. I was a little bit older than most of these men, but I viewed them as adult children. Soon it was time for me to be discharged. I was a free man. I went to college, taking the welding program, which was easy for me because I had been through the navy welding program. Soon I had a real job in a strip mine in Southern Illinois. I would stay there for over twenty years. While at the mines, I was a safety committeeman. It was my job to make sure the men were safe and to settle disputes the men had. Many of them acted like children. I would keep this job for sixteen of the twenty years I was there. On August 19, my world was turned over—the mine closed. A few years before the closure, I had gotten involved in girls' softball. I did this with some reservation. It was then that I realized my own two daughters were excited about softball. Why shouldn't I try it? After the first game, I was hooked. As I watched these five- to seven-year-olds hit that first ball or catch that first fly and see those big eyes and smiles, I knew I was in the right place. I would coach for the next fifteen years till my daughters lost interest in the sport. My next job would take me to the veterans' hospital. There I got attached to the old veterans. I could listen to their stories all night. I would stay there for only two and a half years. I then would take a test for the Department of Corrections. They called me for the job, which I declined the first two times. Finally, they called me to offer me a job at the boot camp. I asked the lady to tell me about the boot camp, and she told me it was for first-time offenders, children from the ages seventeen to thirty-five. Before she could finish, I accepted the job. I still work there. I have been there for almost eight years. I enjoy working with children who are not fortunate enough to have parents as I did or have an uncle Duke or to be on that ship, in the mines, being a coach, at the VA hospital, and the boot camp for a reason. All things happen for a reason. So as I close this, I only have one thing to say: "Put me in, Coach, I'm ready to play!"

Morris Document 41

The Coal Miner's Disease

As I looked into the eyes of Chuck, I saw the disbelief as he had just witnessed a man getting shot. It would turn out he hadn't been shot at all. Chuck had been the victim of some of his own stunts he had pulled over the years. He had many clients, only this time, he had messed with an old coal miner.

My story would begin in January 1977 at a strip mine near the village of Crab Orchard. After being there only a short while, I contracted a disease called coal miner's syndrome. Some of the symptoms of this disease are unstoppable laughter, having deviant thought, and finally that deep desire to get even. I would stay at this job for twenty-plus years till the mine closed in 1996. My disease would lay dormant, only to come to life at times to defend my honor. You see, a coal miner is a special breed. He likes to laugh a lot and seems to be at his best when he laughs a lot, for during these times, he is much more productive. If this is true, I had to be the most productive worker there—*not*! I can't begin to count the hours I spent planning a one-minute stunt, but I feel laughter is the best medicine; we had buckets of it.

We now jump to 1999. I was a brand-new officer at the Dixon Springs Boot Camp. This was a new world for me, so much different from the world of being a welder. I hadn't been there but a few days when this muscled-up guy began to mess with me. I thought he must have worked in a coal mine, but he hadn't. After many of his stunts had been pulled, he would ask me when I was going to get even. I would only reply, "When you play, you must pay." One day after he found out I was a serious mushroom hunter, he came to me and asked me if I would take him hunting with me. As we talked, my disease suddenly came out of remission, and I agreed to take him and set up a date to meet at my house. That night I called a man who had been the best man in my wedding and asked him if he wanted to get involved in a sting operation. He asked what it involved, and I told him, "Me and you, the victim [Chuck], and a blank pistol." He jumped at the chance, for you see, he too was an old coal miner. I told Chuck to be at my house at 7:30. The other guy was to be at the woods at 8:00 a.m. By 8:00 a.m., Chuck and I had been in the woods only a few minutes, when my accomplice drove by. I said, "Oh no, he's not supposed to be here," and I told Chuck to stand still; maybe he would not see us. Chuck hid behind a tree. The man went on by as we had rehearsed. After about a minute, he came to the woods and stopped. He got out of his truck and started up toward us. I told Chuck not to move, to let me do the talking because the old man was crazy. There was no telling what he would do. As many know, Chuck is experienced in martial arts, so I made sure he was some distance behind so he would not kick the crap out of my buddy. As my accomplice approached us, I greeted him. He quickly began to tell me to get off his property. I told him this was not his property. That is when he got loud and began to cuss me. At this point, I removed the pistol from my back pocket and began to slide it up my back. I wanted Chuck to see it. After some arguing, I told him it was not worth someone getting hurt, that we would go to another woods. After that, we started to leave. That is when he cussed me real bad and called me an SOB, so I simply killed him. After only two shots from my blank pistol, my friend lay dead on the floor of the woods. As I turned to look at Chuck, there was disbelief on his face. He could only say, "You stupid SOB." His knees were very shaky. As we stood there, I could not look at him. Finally, Chuck could see my buddy shaking with laughter. That is when I busted my guts. The only thing Chuck could say was, "Boy, you guys play rough." As my buddy got up to leave, I told Chuck that we would go to another, that this one was just my decoy woods. Chuck replied, "I can't walk,"

SUNRISE

for his knees were shaking. Over the remainder of the day, we had a lot of laughter. I told Chuck that the way coal miners fail, they tell things. They don't mean to; they just slip out. I now have learned that when correctional officers are faced with this, they sometimes fail also. Chuck is still a very good friend of mine. I'm sure if I asked anything of him, he would be there to help me. The best thing I like about him is that he is so easy. When you play, you must pay!

Morris Document 42

The Ode to Chuck

Set to the tune of "Big Bad John."

Every morning at the camp, you'd see him arrive—he stood five fee nine inches, weighed 185, kinda broad at the shoulders, narrow at the hip, and everyone knew you didn't give no lip to Big Chuck.

Nobody ever knew where Chuck called home; he just drifted from dorm to dorm, kinda stayed all alone, a little mischievous, and maybe a little shy; and if you spoke at all, you just said hi to Big Chuck.

Some said he came from Shawnee, where he got in a fight over a greased set of keys, and with a crashing blow from his huge right hand, sent a little Bucomb fellow to the promised land. Big Chuck.

So he settled here at the HP. First, he messed with you; now he's messed with me. And if you know me at all, you've probably heard me say that if you're gonna play someday, you'll have to pay. Come here, Chuck.

Then came that day in edge of the woods—when a fellow paid him back and he paid him back pretty good. Shots were fired and hearts beat fast, and everyone thought the guy had breathed his last, especially Chuck.

Then with sacks and sticks, they started to another woods. Chuckie yelled out, "Hey, hang on! I'm not walking so very good. My knees are a knockin', and my shorts are kinda soggy—I'm a little confused, and I'm feelin kinda groggy." Big Chuck.

SUNRISE

So if you ever venture down to the HP, you better take a glance behind thee, 'cause lurking in shadows will be the blue-eyed devil, and we all know the fellow just ain't level. Big Chuck.

You see, they never reopened that mushroom pit. They just placed a little sign out in front of it; these few words were written out in front of that patch: "Out in these here woods—is where Chuckie met his match—Big Chuck."

Author chooses to remain unknown. Any reproduction of this document is encouraged. For more information, visit me at my website, GetEven.com.

Morris Document 43

Those Darn Nailheads

When I was a young boy, I was in 4-H. This club was based on agriculture and things around the farm. Some would raise calves or hogs for projects. One summer we had the meeting at my dad's farm. After the meeting came the recreation. This day we would play chain tag, a game where you would tag the one you were after, and the last one standing was the winner. My dad had this huge barn. On one side the roof was steep, while on the other side it was sloped and not so steep. Copper guy wire for the lightning arresters ran from the ground rod up to the peak of the roof to guard against lightning. I had gone to the sloped side and pulled myself to the peak. As I sat there, I watched all the boys running around to catch me. Suddenly my neighbor saw me and started that long climb up the sloped side of the barn. When I saw him, I started letting myself down the steep side. He thought I was sliding down the barn roof. As he reached the peak, he slid on the roof. I will never forget the look on his face as he passed me that day. You see, this barn roof was put on with lead nailheads that protruded from the roof. You could hear him hit the heads as his butt raked over the roof. His pants were torn open, and his butt was bleeding. This was the high point of our meeting, for he had provided the entertainment.

Morris Document 44

The Smoke Bomb

Over the twenty-plus years I worked in a strip mine, there were many funny stories to tell. One of my favorite included the story about a smoke bomb, a foreman, and a bunch of gloomy coal miners. I remember that morning just as if it were yesterday. It was 1985, a gloomy overcast day. We hadn't seen the sun in two days. Have you ever noticed what effect the sun has on a person's mood? As we left the bathhouse that morning, a man gave me a smoke bomb and said, "I thought you could have some fun with this." I slipped it in my pocket and got in the van that carried us to our work site. I ran a huge D-9L bulldozer used in mine reclamation. As we drove to the area where we would work that day, I tried to think how I would use this smoke bomb. As we arrived at the work site, my foreman arrived as usual. He was met by a bunch of long aced coal miners that weren't really in any mood to be there, let alone work. Then I noticed he wasn't driving his usual truck. This day he was driving the head repair supervisor's truck. My devious mind began to spin. He sat in his truck, looking over some paperwork that he used to assign each of us jobs that day. As he came to the van to give out the work, I asked, "Did they get that gas leak fixed on Paul's truck?" He said he wasn't aware of a gas leak. He then said he had forgotten some paperwork and he would be right back. As he went back to his truck, I jumped from the van and went around the back, lit the smoke bomb, and tossed it under the front end of his truck, and I went back in the van. Only the guy that gave me the bomb saw me leave the van. As he approached the van, I could see the smoke starting to come from beneath the truck. That particular morning, it was muddy. We had rain the last couple of days. Suddenly, the driver of the van saw the smoke. He yelled, "Fire!"

My foreman yelled, "Oh my god! Paul's truck!" He dropped his clipboard and ran to the truck and dropped to his knees and shot under the truck. As he got under the truck, he saw the smoke bomb and crawled back out with mud all over him. Immediately the van erupted in laughter as he cussed. As he searched the van to find the culprit of this stunt, our eyes met, and he called my name at the top of his voice. I guess I must have looked sort of guilty. He then surprised all of us. He busted into laughter, which made us laugh even harder. As he wiped the mud off his pants, he said, "In all my years of working at this mine, this is the best prank I have seen. I may take me twenty years, but I'll get even with you." That made us howl even harder. After we wiped the tears from our eyes, and he wiped the mud from his clothes, we went to work. Every time one of us would see the other, the laughter would erupt again. Have you ever noticed how much more productive you are when you are lighthearted?

That day we moved double the amount of dirt we had the day before. As for the foreman, every time our paths crossed, he said, "If it takes another twenty years, I will get even." Of course, as he said this, he could not keep his composure.

This is just one of the many stories that took place over my twenty-plus years at that strip mine. These memories are like old pictures we all have. We need to blow the dust from them every now and then when we need a good laugh!

Morris Document 45

Hot-Dogger

It was November 1973. My ship was broke down near Faslane, Scotland. We would spend the next three months awaiting orders as to where they would send us. Scotland is a very beautiful country with beautiful people. They had made us feel very welcome, and we had been accepted in this small inlet city. There wasn't much to do for these people except go to work and then go to the pub then do the same thing over the next day. We were anchored out in the harbor because we had no power. We would run motor boats to and from the pier when we wanted to go over, as they say. Their main food were the fish and chips; chips were fried potatoes, which were very tasty. There seemed to be no crime here. You could walk the streets with no worry. It felt really safe, unlike the feeling you have when you walk the streets Stateside.

One day a friend of mine by the name of Rob Hudson—but we all called him Hot-Dogger—came to the shop I ran and asked me if I had any old welding rods he could have. When I asked him what he needed them for, he simply replied it was none of my business. I gave him a fifty-pound box of welding rods that had gotten wet and we could no longer use. For the next three nights after work, he would sharpen these rods to a fine point. I asked him what he was doing, and again he replied it was none of my business. One afternoon he came to me and asked me to get a loaf of bread and meet him on top of the hangar by the bay. Again as before, he told me it was none of my business. I got the bread and met him on the main deck and started the climb to the top of the hangar bay. He was ahead of me with the box of welding rods on his broad shoulders. Once we were up there, he instructed me to start throwing the bread. I looked at him as if he had lost his mind. Then I saw what he was doing. As I threw the bread, the seagulls would try to catch the bread. He then would throw the welding rods at them. As I watched him, I had to laugh, for the rods he had taken three afternoons to sharpen were gone in five minutes without the first casualty. We sat up there and laughed about how ridiculous we had to look on top of the hangar bay that day.

This one man made my four-year stint in the navy so much easier. He made me laugh daily about something. I don't think being away from home would have been so tolerable without his being there to break the boredom. This same man would carry me around Africa on up into the Red Sea and the many other places around this world. The good Lord put this great friend in my path to give me joy on my journeys. We still keep in touch after all these years. He is still as crazy as ever. He is my friend Hot-Dogger.

Morris Document 46

Just One More Peep

As a child I grew up on a 320-acre farm in deep Southern Illinois. We did not have a great deal. It took everything Dad could make to make ends meet. Dad worked during the day as a construction worker and worked as a farmer in his spare time. He also ran five hundred chickens so he could sell eggs to the various restaurants in the area. Do you know how many eggs five hundred chickens can lay? We had to hand-wash each and every egg and put them into twenty-four-dozen crates. He also ran a herd of cattle as well as hogs, so you can see he was a very busy man. He also had three sons to raise. I still to this day don't know how he managed this all, but he did with not the first complaint.

    My mother was outnumbered as well. She too did all this work without complaining. My mother was a saint. She had to be with us three boys always pulling some sort of prank on each other. We didn't have many toys, so we had to improvise to make our own entertainment. We would saw out guns to play army with or make our fishing poles out of cane we would cut down by the creek. But we were happy and content in our little world on the farm. Many times we would get on Mom's nerves to the point she would say, "Just wait till your dad gets home." We dreaded that so much, for we knew we had crossed that line. Dad was an expert at busting your hind end. He would get the message across. It wasn't the whipping that bothered me as much as the wait; that was the bad part. We all had to pull together to make this operation work. Somehow we did make it, and it was these hard days on the farm that would develop a solid work ethic that we all carried into adulthood.

During these times, we lived in a small three-room house. We all slept in one bedroom with two full-sized beds. One Tuesday night, which was Dad's local meeting night, we boys were cutting up as we usually did. Dad came home with dried concrete all over him. He ate his supper, then it was time for bed. We boys weren't ready for bed but went through the motion as Dad had requested. In Dad's house, when Mom and Dad went to bed, everybody went to bed. Dad warned us two times to lie down and go to sleep, till finally he said, "If I hear one peep out of you boys, I'll bust three hind ends." The room went deathly quiet and stayed that way. I had to sleep in the middle because I was the youngest. I lay there for a while till I made a huge mistake. I simply went, "Peep."

I had never seen my dad move as fast as he did that night. He jumped from that bed, stripped those covers off, and had three hind ends busted before you could turn around. Then after the smoke had cleared, he told us to pick those covers up and go to sleep. This was when the elbows and knees pounded me from both sides. I still think to this day that Dad was laughing about that night, for he has a wonderful sense of humor. I think often of the fun times in that old three-room house. Part of it was used when he built the new one on that very site. God had to smile down on us during these times, probably due to my mother's prayers that she said day and night. Much laughter was held in that old house; that was back when life was simple. I like to visit that old house every now and then in my mind when my life gets so hectic, then I can cope better. Just one more peep!

Morris Document 47

My Smokey Mountain Gift

Christmas 2009 found my family of ten in a huge cabin nestled eight hundred feet up a mountain near Pigeon Forge, Tennessee. The real story began back in January when I planned this vacation and had told my wife to also plan her tie off during this time. We also told our three daughters and their husbands and one boyfriend to join on this trip. We were to buy only for the grandchildren for the gift was the trip itself. Time passed, and finally it was time to leave. So here we go on our car caravan headed for Tennessee. The cabin my wife had rented was wonderful, with four bedroom and four baths complete with hot tub and a pool table. Also near was an indoor swimming pool. The view was fantastic. You could see for miles either balcony of our two-story cabin. During the day we would browse in the various shops around Gatlinburg or Pigeon Forge. The evenings were filled with laughter as we watched our grandchildren open their gifts and run around this huge cabin. I had told them all to bring no gifts on this trip, but they had brought me a gift they had bought themselves. The laughter and love we shared blessed my heart and brought tears to my eyes. Each morning would find me on the balcony, eagerly waiting for God to show his face as the sun rose over these beautiful lands. There was not the first crossword during the entire trip. It was a perfect time we shared together.

Few times in life do we experience perfect harmony as we did during our five days in paradise. God certainly blessed this trip for us all. Many times we do not appreciate our loved ones with our busy schedules we all keep, so this special vacation will always have a special place in my heart. The cabin was quite expensive, but dollars mean nothing to me as I experienced the joy on the faces of my family on this wonderful vacation. Gifts are wonderful things, but things are merely things. The gifts they had brought were themselves all wrapped in love. As I look on this vacation, I cannot think of a single thing I would change. This wonderful time bound us together as a family. Money could never buy the love experienced by us all as we shared one another during this time. My family's presence made my Smokey Mountain gift special in my heart.

Morris Document 48

My Favorite Christmas

Of all the favorite Christmases over my lifetime, one sticks out in my mind. The year was 1973, and I was in the navy, on a destroyer off the coast of Cape Town, South Africa. Through this cruise, my wife and I had sent cassette tapes back and forth so we could hear each other's voices. About a week after Christmas, a tape arrived from her, but this was not your regular tape. It was a tape of Christmas at my parents' home. Everyone was there except me. As I played the tape in my repair shop, I could close my eyes and visualize where everyone sitting, and I could hear the laughter and the sound of packages being unwrapped. As I cried, I was happy because I suddenly realized how important each and every one of them was to me. I often drift back in time when the hustle and bustle of Christmas gets to me and remember what Christmas is to me.

We sometimes forget what Christmas is all about with all the commercialism and spending money for things we really do not need in the first place. Christmas is supposed to be celebrating the birth of Christ, but we oftentimes forget this. For me it took this period of separation to show me all the wonders God has tried to show me all along, but I was too busy to notice. I feel God was sitting on my shoulder that dark night at sea off the coast of South Africa.

Morris Document 49

1999—a Year of Changes

The year 1999; it's hard to believe, isn't it? This has certainly been a year full of changes for the Morris household. It is so hard for me to grasp the idea that we are about to enter into a new century, but like it or not, we have no choice. Our one simple lifestyle has been scattered about by living in different locations, different schedules, different shifts, and let us not leave different on-call schedules.

The year 1999 also marked the first year since 1979 that the Morris house was inhabited by only three people. The year 1999 was also the first year that Mom and Dad had to face the fact that two of their children had moved away from home. Of course, Amanda had been away from home, but she was only thirty-five minutes away. This move, to Dad, seemed so far away. Amanda and Nicki's education is very important not only to them but also to Mom and Dad, as well as Heather. Many times distance between people that love each other in the long run brings them much closer together. As I look at what Amanda and Nicki have learned, I see not only college classes and credits. I also see the lessons of independence, of learning to stand on their own two feet, and of having to make decisions for themselves. These are lessons college can't teach. I am proud of both of you.

Heather has adapted well to being the only child in the Morris house. She is maturing so fast that it scares me. She is no longer a little girl; she is a beautiful young lady. I really believe she misses her sisters a lot, as I am sure they miss her. Heather will go into high school next year. That in itself does not seem possible. I guess I am the one who doesn't want to turn my kids loose. But whether it may be children moving away to college or kids moving on to high school, just as 1999 is rolling to 2000, we cannot stop the clock.

My pretty wife, Rene, has felt the effect of the changes I have mentioned. She is the one that seems to catch all the phone calls both at work and at home and is required to know all the answers at once. That's not to mention cook, clean, keep the books, wash the dog, raise a daughter, put up with a husband, put up with Marge, and the thousand other things that come up on a daily basis she has to deal with. The other thing she does is to be on call. This has been a very stressful change for my wife. Many days she goes on little or no sleep, and what sleep she does get is often interrupted. *I hate call.*

As for me, 1999 has also been a year of change. In March I started a new job with the state of Illinois at the boot camp in Dixon Springs. This was more of a change for me than any of you will ever know. The first three months I had to make myself go to work, because I wasn't sure this was for me. I am now adjusted to it, and I will be fine. I have learned to appreciate my family more, especially my children. As I talk to these kids and listen to their stories, they can tear your heart out, and you quickly come to realize that they simply had no raising. Granted they did the crimes that put them where they are, but they didn't, in most cases, have the support of a family we take for granted. So working there has made me appreciate my children and see them in a different light.

I can't fail to mention Chris and Ryan. These guys have also felt the changes of this year. Being away from someone you care about takes some adjustment. Being apart can be hard, but as I said before, it can be a good thing as well.

I'll close this now. These were just a few things I've had on my mind. I'll be saying how much I love all of you and how important you all are to me. Have a merry Christmas and a great 2000. Wow, THAT SOUNDS WEIRD!

Morris Document 52

The Stranger

Recently I finished my first ever book. It had taken me twenty-seven years to complete this book, with many sleepless nights and adventures along the way. Now came the huge task of somehow getting it edited and published. I had given a few copies to friends and coworkers and had been encouraged to publish this book. But getting a book published is a huge task, and I knew nothing about it. One day, about two weeks after completion, I was at work at the boot camp when I saw a strange man pull up on the grounds. As he got out of his car, I noticed he was wearing a state ID, so I approached him for identification. It turned out he was the chaplain for corrections. We hit it from the start and soon were locked in conversation. I noticed his name was the same as a man I knew at the Vienna prison, so I asked him if he was kin to this man. He told me this man was his brother. I then asked if his brother was the one who had written a book on his life, and he said he was. After several more questions, I asked where he had it published. He then blew me away when he said, "I published it myself."

As I stood there in front of a man I had just met, I realized God had put us on a collision course that cool day in December. As I told him about my book, he became very interested and would like to read it sometime. As fate would have it, I had a copy in my car. This man then told me that with the way I had described my writing, I could have not one but two books. To this I was astounded and could not speak as he thumbed through the pages. Sometimes in life our paths cross with some of the most interesting people. Many times we are so busy to notice these angels that are right in front of our faces. These opportunities will pass just as time and years do, only to be lost forever. Seize your opportunities as they come before you, and you can reap the blessings as I did.

Morris Document 56

Solid Ground

When life's trials are over, when I finally reach the end,

When I look back at all those wasted years, I'll think of my best friend—you see, Jesus came to me one night, when I was lost and so alone.

He reached down with his saving hand and said, "Son, I'm going to take you home!"

Chorus:

> Well, he picked me up to never let me down—you see, Jesus took my old struggling soul, and he put my feet on solid ground. He can pick you up—to never let you down—Jesus can take your struggling soul and put your feet on solid ground!

You see, I am struggling daily with a bushel basket full of sin—but Jesus took my old long face, and upon it he set a grin. You know I love a lot of laughter. You know I love to joke around—now I know when I leave this place, I'm gonna light on solid ground.

Chorus

You know I used to walk only with my pockets stuffed full of pride, but now I walk a different road 'cause I've got Jesus by my side.

You see, I used to walk in darkness, knowing full well I wasn't right, but now I walk a lighted path 'cause my Jesus holds the light.

Chorus

So if you struggle daily with a bushel basket full of sin—you may be like Nicodemus—you must be born again, and if you're walking on this old earth and you're always feeling down, trust in God, and you can put your feet on solid ground!

Chorus

He picked me up to never let me down—Jesus took this old struggling soul, and he put my feet on solid ground. He can pick you up—he'll never let you down. Jesus can take your old struggling soul and put your feet on solid ground—yes, he can put your feet on solid ground!

Morris Document 57

Angry and Dejected

When angry and dejected, I'll go for a little walk. That's when I get my head straight, and with my Lord, I'll talk—you see, Jesus came to me one night and said, "Son, I'm gonna set you free—simply lay this world aside and come and follow me!"

Chorus:

> 'Cause I can hear him in my laughter—I can feel him in my pain. I can hear his voice in the thunder—I can taste him in the rain. He said, "You gonna live forever in this heavenly eternity—simply lay this world aside and come and follow me."

Well, the first road I had chosen seemed a little bit rough—I couldn't help but wonder if I was made of the right stuff. But as I pondered on my thoughts, it came so clear to me, that he wanted not a quarter or a half—he wanted all of me.

Chorus

Now my life is so much richer even when it rains. I now hear a lot of laughter—where I once felt a lot of pain—and when I get dejected, I get my shoes on and walk. That's when I get my head so straight, and with my Lord I talk!

Yes, I can hear him in my laughter—I can feel him in my pain. I can hear his voice when the thunder rolls—I can taste him in the rain. He said, "You're gonna live forever in a heavenly eternity—simply lay this world aside and come and follow me."

He said, "Won't you simply lay your world aside and come and follow me?"

Morris Document 58

Up Comes the Son

October 29, 2007

I rise up early every morning and step outside to greet the day. My world it seemed so dark and so dreary that I could not find my way.

My steps are blinded by the darkness, my pathways hold only despair—but as the sun splits that eastern sky, hope, only hope, is everywhere.

Chorus:

> Up comes the Son, my life seems much brighter
> Up comes the Son, my fears are gone
> And my paths, my paths seem so much clearer
> All because, all because up comes the Son!

When I was young, I met the master. I walked with him along life's ways—but as I grew, the world took over and my life, my life was led astray.

Till at last one sunny morning I looked straight upon his face—and now my life it has new meaning all because of repent—up comes the Son.

Chorus

    Now I am older and much wiser—a wife and girls to call my own. A fine grandson to share my life with—I owe this all to him, up comes the Son.

Chorus

Author's wife Rene
From left to right: Nicki, Amanda, Neather

His name was River

Seldom in life does someone enters your life that transforms your life and adds joy to the whole family. Along comes June 9, 2012. River has brought so much joy and laughter to our family. He is the family clown. He can make you smile simply by walking in the room. Now grandpa has two wonderful grandsons to spoil. When I look back I have to wonder how we made it without him

They called him River!

From top to Bottom
River
Chloe
Halle
Noah

They called her Chloe Bug

Along comes June 25, 2010, the third grandchild comes on the scene. She is petite and perfect. Now grandma has two granddaughters to spoil. She could break your heart with those big eyes. Now her brother has someone to grow up with. She has brought so much joy to our family. I would work three jobs to give these grandbabies what they wanted.

They called Chloe Bug